Dear Reader,

Home, family, community and love. These are the values we cherish most in our lives—the ideals that ground us, comfort us, move us. They certainly provide the perfect inspiration around which to build a romance collection that will touch the heart.

Each of these special stories in the Harlequin Heartwarming collection is a wholesome, heartfelt romance imbued with the traditional values so important to you. They are books you can share proudly with friends and family. And the authors featured in this collection are some of the most talented storytellers writing today, including favorites such as Laura Abbot, Roz Denny Fox, Janice Kay Johnson and Irene Hannon. We've selected these stories especially for you based on their overriding qualities of emotion and tenderness, and they center around your favorite themes—children, weddings, second chances, the reunion of families, the quest to find a true home and, of course, sweet romance.

So curl up in your favorite chair, relax and prepare for a heartwarming reading experience!

Sincerely,

The Editors

ROXANNE RUSTAND

lives in the country with her husband and a menagerie of pets, many of whom find their way into her books. Roxanne has a master's degree in nutrition, and until leaving her position to write full-time, she worked as a clinical dietitian at a residential psychiatric facility. Now you'll find her writing at home in her jammies, surrounded by three dogs begging for treats, or out in the barn with the horses. Her favorite time of all is when her kids are home—though all three are now busy with college and jobs. *RT Book Reviews* nominated her for a Career Achievement Award in 2005, and she won the magazine's award for Best Superromance of 2006. Roxanne loves to hear from readers! Her mailing address is P.O. Box 2550, Cedar Rapids, Iowa, 52406-2550. You can also contact her at www.roxannerustand.com, www.shoutlife.com/roxannerustand, on Facebook and on Twitter.

HEARTWARMING

Home at Blackberry Hill

—

Roxanne Rustand

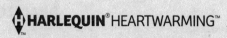

Recycling programs
for this product may
not exist in your area.

ISBN-13: 978-0-373-36760-3

Home at Blackberry Hill

Copyright © 2011 by Roxanne Rustand

Originally published as A Temporary Arrangement

Copyright © 2006 by Roxanne Rustand

Printed in U.S.A.

Home at Blackberry Hill

This book is dedicated to the memory
of my dear mother,
who always encouraged me to be a writer.

CHAPTER ONE

ABBY CAHILL breathed in the crisp, pine-scented air, then stepped inside Blackberry Hill Memorial Hospital to start a new chapter in her life.

The retiring director of nursing, Grace Fisher-Edwards, met her inside the door with a broad smile. "I was afraid the tourist traffic would slow you down, but you're right on time." She ushered Abby down the hall to her office. "June can be a real bear around here."

Abby laughed. "On par with five o'clock rush hour in Detroit, except the scenery is much, much prettier."

"If you can see past the vehicles, that is." Grace snorted as she settled behind her cluttered desk and shifted a stack of files to one side. "During the summer, our population triples."

"And I think every last one of those tourists is on Main right now." Grinning, Abby searched through her shoulder bag for her notebook and a pen. "I sure wish I could've come a few days earlier, but our nursing students' graduation was on Saturday and then I still had to pack."

"You must be exhausted."

"No...though I do look forward to settling into my new place." Abby sat back in her chair and uncapped her pen.

Grace's eyes filled with concern. "I gather you haven't stopped by the Hawthorne Apartments."

"Not yet." Abby flipped open the notebook, her pen poised over its pristine surface. "Meeting with you was my biggest priority, believe me."

"The manager tried to call you yesterday. He even called the hospital, hoping Erin or I would know how to reach you."

Abby stilled. "My home phone was disconnected yesterday morning, and I have a new cell. But there shouldn't be a problem—I've signed a lease."

"There was a fire over the weekend."

"Oh, my," Abby said faintly. "Was anyone hurt?"

"No, but half your building was gutted,

leaving seven families homeless…and now you, I guess." Grace pushed a piece of paper across the desk. "I've done some checking, but there aren't many apartments in this area. I'm afraid those displaced renters have already taken what little there was."

"I'm glad I left most of my things in storage for the summer." Abby considered the situation for a moment. "Maybe I can find a cabin to rent. Or even a motel, until the apartment building's livable."

"I'm not sure it ever will be." Grace worried her lower lip. "We've heard rumors for years about the owner wanting to raze the entire complex so he can put up fancy condos."

Dread settled in the pit of Abby's stomach. "What are my options?"

"Even vacation lodging is hard to come by during the tourist season. Most places are reserved months ahead. But I did find a few possibilities." Grace's dubious expression didn't bode well. "And you're sure welcome to stay with Warren and me. We leave on our wedding trip in the morning, but you could stay on through tomorrow night."

"You two just got married—what?—this

past weekend. I'd hate to move in on you, especially with you getting ready to leave."

"I wish I could offer you more, but my house has been sold and the contractors start on Warren's place Thursday morning. Once they tear up the plumbing and old wiring, I'm afraid it won't be habitable until they finish in July."

"Please, don't even give it a thought. I'm only here for a few months, so I can make do with just about anything."

She scanned Grace's list. A motel along the lake with weekly rates. Several small resorts with cabins. A furnished house for rent.

But the bigger issue was her new job and the fact that Grace—the person best suited to groom her temporary successor—was leaving town tomorrow.

"I'd rather spend as much time as I can with you. I can figure out my housing problems later."

"Are you sure?" Grace sounded doubtful. "With your background, you should have no difficulty taking over. Erin tells me you were a top student when you two were in training together. And your article in the *Journal of Hospital Nursing* last year was amazing."

"Psychology of Patient Care in the Low Income Setting" represented three years of research and had taken her at least sixteen drafts. Reprints were now required reading in several nursing programs across the United States and would be included in a college textbook released next spring.

But that article—and the others she'd written—provided no more practical knowledge on running a nursing department than *Wuthering Heights.*

"As you know, it's been a while since I worked in a hospital." Abby managed a light laugh. "I may have been teaching nursing for years, but I'm going to need every bit of advice you can offer."

"And I'll be glad to give it. But first, I really think you'd better take a few hours to look for a place to stay." Grace glanced at her watch. "Come back at, say, four o'clock?"

"But my orientation—"

"Don't worry. I'll still be here when you get back and we can stay as late as we need to." Tapping the files on her desk, Grace gave her a grandmotherly smile. "Last month, we revised the facility-wide policy and procedure manuals, and they'll explain every last detail of running this place. Coupled with the files I've pulled together for you, you'll have everything you need to know."

Updated policy and procedure manuals. Complete files. The words were a balm to Abby's left-brained soul. She felt the tension in her shoulders ease. "Sounds like this should be a smooth transition, then. Thanks."

"Everyone is looking forward to having you here." The hint of admiration in Grace's voice was unmistakable. "And though you'll only be here for a short while, I know you'll be a great asset."

Three months, to be precise, until the new permanent director of nursing arrived. Surely she could handle a small, quiet hospital like this one for three months, and the experience would be perfect research for her next article.

Abby smiled. "I can't tell you how much I've looked forward to enjoying the slower pace up here."

"Slower pace?" Grace repeated, a faint, enigmatic smile on her lips. "I think we'll have a lot to discuss before this day is over."

AFTER TWO HOURS of fruitless searching, Abby realized just how right Grace had been about this busy resort town.

It had all seemed so simple while she was packing. After the graduation ceremony, a formal tea at her mother's Rosewood Lakes estate and a quiet farewell gathering at her father's country club, she'd savored every moment of the beautiful drive north to the quaint Wisconsin town of Blackberry Hill.

She hadn't been prepared for the bumper-to-propeller traffic during the final two hours of the trip or the crowds attending the Blackberry Hill Arts Festival. Not to mention there wasn't a single place to stay within fifty miles.

Every possibility on Grace's list was filled, along with three others she'd found in the local newspaper.

Scooping her hair away from her damp forehead, she tugged at the collar of her limp cotton blouse and knocked on the door of her last resort: an old house with a sagging front porch at the end of Bailey Street.

A minute later the door swung open to reveal a bony and bent eighty-something man with a scowl on his face.

"I'm not buying anything," he snapped.

"I'm here about the room," she said as he started to close the door. "Please—is it still available?"

The man in front of her was as charming as his advertisement.

She'd seen the scrawled note tacked to the bulletin board of the grocery store downtown, hidden beneath a flyer advertising Lawn Care—Good Rates.

"Efficiency available by the month. Private entrance. No smoking. No drinking. No guests of the opposite sex. No pets. No noise. One month rent deposit. Hubert L. Bickham, 234 Bailey Street."

Hubert L. Bickham's scowl deepened as he studied her from head to foot with narrowed eyes. "I don't allow any hanky-panky. No trouble." He jerked a thumb toward the side of the house, where she'd seen exterior stairs leading to the second floor of the small one-and-a-half-story house. "Those stairs go right past my bedroom, and any noise wakes me up. So no tromping up them stairs at all hours, missy."

Despite the heat, the frustration and her need to get back to the hospital, Abby had to struggle to keep a straight face.

No one had ever accused her of leading a wild life.

She held up her hand in a Scout salute. "I swear."

He chewed at his lower lip. "You got the deposit?"

"Yes, sir."

"Ain't a big town, if you're lookin' for work. You got a job?"

"Blackberry Hill Memorial Hospital. I'm the new director of nursing. The *interim* director, I should say," Abby added carefully.

He appeared mollified at that. "Grace's job."

"Exactly. Last month I leased one of the Hawthorne Apartments near the hospital but—"

"Fire, first floor." He folded his arms across his thin chest and gave her a long, skeptical look. "They checked you out before letting you sign?"

"They did," Abby assured him. "Credit check, work history. Everything."

He thought for a while, searching her face. "I suppose you can have the room, long as you understand the rules and pay on time."

Suppressing the impulse to kiss his whiskery cheek, she quickly read the contract and signed her name, then wrote a check for two months' rent. "You won't regret this. I promise."

He appeared to regret it within minutes—glaring at her from his front window as she lugged her suitcase and several boxes up the sidewalk and around to the stairs. He thumped on his ceiling with—she suspected—a broom handle when one of the boxes slipped from her grasp and hit the floor.

Her new landlord appeared to have a major personality disorder. The apartment was cramped and dark. Yet she wouldn't inconvenience Grace and she'd just bought herself time to find a better place. How hard could that be?

Two weeks later she knew. Finding a better place wasn't hard. It was *impossible.* And working in an idyllic north woods town certainly didn't give her tranquility. Not when she was overseeing the nursing staff of a hospital that had been on the brink of closure less than a year ago.

She'd talked to Grace for hours on her first evening in town. The older woman had even stopped in at the hospital the next morning before she and Warren flew south. She'd run a tight ship and had left her office in perfect order, but every day brought new challenges given the tight budget and shortage of nurses.

"Bad day, professor?" Erin Reynolds, the hospital administrator, smiled sympathetically as she watched Abby pore over the nurses' work schedule on her desk.

"Interesting." Abby grinned back at her.

After graduating together with bachelor's degrees in nursing, they'd gone their separate ways—Erin had eventually gone back to school for a degree in hospital administration, while Abby had chosen graduate school and a career in teaching at the college level.

They'd kept in touch through Christmas cards and occasional emails, though, and Erin had been the one to let Abby know about this temporary position.

"I just need a magic wand and a few more nurses," Abby continued. "Marcia's home with strep throat. Carl's on vacation until Monday. Gwen agreed to pull a double shift today, but I'm trying to avoid that, because she works tomorrow, too."

Erin came farther in and wearily rested

both hands on the back of a chair. Five months pregnant, she was as lovely as ever with her short, glossy dark hair and delicate features, if somewhat drawn and pale. "Any luck with the ad?"

"A half dozen calls and several applications."

"Good." Erin stifled a yawn. "I've asked Madge to run it in the Green Bay and Milwaukee papers this weekend, too."

Erin was just two years older than Abby, and they'd hit it off from the first time they'd met. Now, Abby looked at her old friend with growing concern.

The hospital was in the midst of renovation and expansion efforts that hadn't been going smoothly. With the three children Erin had adopted before marrying Dr. Reynolds last winter, her job and her pregnancy, she looked ready to drop in her tracks.

Dr. Jill Edwards, on the other hand, was due the month after Erin, but she barely showed yet and seemed to have boundless energy. Though without other children to contend with, she probably got much more rest.

"So, is it true you and Connor have never had any weekend time alone?" Abby asked.

Erin and Connor had flown to the Bahamas in late January for a beachside wedding with all three children as attendants. "Not even on your wedding trip?"

"We had adjoining rooms."

"Not quite the same," Abby said. "I'm thinking you need some absolute peace and quiet. This weekend."

Erin snorted. "I don't think that'll happen. Our sitter is off on her senior class trip this week. Connor's on call this weekend and he's also covering Jill's practice while she's out of town. He'll probably end up sleeping at the hospital, so it'll be just me, the kids and my round-the-clock morning sickness. I can't believe the nausea has continued past the first trimester."

"So this could be a weekend to pamper yourself. Maybe I could take the kids—"

"You?" Erin's eyes were round. "Are you feeling okay?"

"How hard could it be?" She'd gone out for pizza a couple times with the Reynolds crew, and she'd also been to a few of the boys' baseball games. The three kids all seemed, well, manageable enough for an afternoon.

"This is so sweet of you. A whole weekend to myself just sounds like *heaven*."

Abby had meant to volunteer for a few hours, but she couldn't resist Erin's gratitude. "Whatever I might've said about lacking maternal instincts, I could do it. I'm a nurse, after all. We're nurturing types." Was she? Her ex-fiancé, Jared, sure hadn't thought so. "And heaven knows, I owe you," she added. "Coming up here is the perfect opportunity for some practical experience before I start teaching again."

Abby ignored a sudden vision of her land-lord Hubert's reaction to all of this. "You could sleep in. Relax."

"As much as I'd love it, I'm afraid the kids are really energetic. I swear, sometimes they could wear out the patience of a saint."

The children had been adopted shortly before Erin's first husband left her for another woman. All three had come from troubled backgrounds, but Erin had already done wonders with them. Surely she was exaggerating.

"And I'm *not* exaggerating," Erin added dryly. "No matter what I tell them, they'll push the limit with anyone new—that's why

Haley is still our one and only babysitter. The others refuse to come back."

"If I can handle this hospital job, I can handle three kids. And if things get really wild, you're only a phone call away," Abby added firmly.

"Well…" Erin hesitated for a moment, then dissolved into laughter. "Deal. Though I'll understand completely, if you decide to give them back early."

"Not a chance. The boys, Lily and I are going to have a *great* time."

WHAT EXACTLY, did one do with three kids under the age of eleven to make sure they had a "great time"?

Connor dropped them off after supper on Friday. Abby took them to a movie, for pizza, then finally to the video store on Main Street.

There, eleven-year-old Drew had argued for renting some sort of video game for the Xbox he'd brought along. Eight-year-old Tyler had begged for a different game, one Drew said was dumb. And ten-year-old Lily had shyly asked for an old worn-out Harry Potter movie she'd seen at least a million times, according to Tyler.

Abby's plans for holding a vote fizzled when the boys stood toe-to-toe and both proclaimed it was *their* turn to choose. Abby ended up renting all three and praying for peace.

Now, back at the stairway to her small upstairs apartment, Abby held a finger to her lips. "My landlord is elderly and needs his sleep. We have to be very quiet, okay?"

Lily nodded and tiptoed up. Tyler stumbled on the third step and yelped as his knee struck the edge of the riser. Drew, distracted by a motorcycle coming down the street, bumbled into him and said a few words he must have learned in inner city Chicago during his earlier days. The video he'd been carrying bounced down the stairs to the grass.

Sure enough, the lights in Hubert's first-floor bedroom blazed on a second later and he appeared at his window to peer out into the dark.

"Sorry, Mr. Bickham," Abby called.

Shooing the kids ahead of her, she held a finger to her lips again and gave them a conspiratorial smile. "He's got very, very good ears," she whispered. "Let's pretend we're secret agents and see how quiet we can be."

Upstairs, the kids seemed surprised by the efficiency's small living area, dominated by a threadbare couch and single chair. The tiny kitchenette in one corner. The queen-size bed she'd angled into another corner, and had covered with her jewel-toned quilt and shams in an effort to make the place more homey.

"This is real pretty," Lily murmured. "But there's no place for us to sleep."

"That's why Connor dropped off your sleeping bags and duffels this morning. I figure you can each camp in a different corner. You're welcome to make tents out of chairs and my extra blankets."

Tyler grinned. "Cool."

"I'm over by the TV, and I get it first," Drew announced. He pawed through one of the duffels and pulled out a black plastic box with cords and controllers dangling from it like an electronic octopus. In seconds he was behind the small TV, figuring out the connections.

"That's not *fair*," Tyler complained. "We didn't even draw for it."

Draw for it? Abby realized she should have managed the first TV rights equitably. "How about giving Drew an hour, then you and Lily can draw straws for who goes next?"

Lily, who'd settled on the couch with a Harry Potter hardcover book that weighed almost as much as she did, shot Abby a look of gratitude, then dropped her gaze to the open book in her lap.

Tyler stuck out his lower lip. "Drew's always first, just 'cause he's bigger. And if Lily wins, that's not fair, 'cause her dumb movie lasts *forever.*"

Reminded of her one—and only—disastrous babysitting job as a teen, Abby smiled. "Then how about helping me bake some cookies while you wait? You could be the one to decorate them before they go in the oven."

The television blared to life—a cacophony of gunshots and screams that nearly shook the rafters before Drew found the volume button on the remote.

Startled, Lily jerked and her heavy book slid to the floor.

"Watch out, Drew. Wake up the dead, will you?" Tyler snapped.

And from downstairs they heard muffled

yelling...then the *thud! thud! thud!* of Hubert's broom handle beneath them.

Abby managed a reassuring smile as she motioned with her hands for quiet. They were good, normal kids. They couldn't help making noise. But this whole idea had obviously been a mistake.

She already knew she'd be hearing from Hubert in the morning...and the news wouldn't be good.

CHAPTER TWO

DELAYING HER INEVITABLE confrontation with Hubert, Abby bustled around her little kitchen, cleaning up after feeding the kids her favorite malted-milk waffles, scrambled eggs with cheese and fresh-squeezed orange juice.

They'd all been restless last night and had finally dozed off at the end of Lily's movie, but for some inexplicable reason they were all awake by six…their occasional arguments or bursts of laughter bringing energy and excitement to the apartment and making her laugh.

But Hubert would be waiting for the sound of footsteps coming down the stairs. And then he'd be on his front porch when she came around the house, ready to complain about her latest Noise Infraction. Hubert, she thought grimly as she dried the final piece of silverware, needed a life.

"Now, we've got two choices," she said as

she wiped the last of the crumbs off the counter. "It's beautiful outside, seventy degrees and sunny. We could stay here and watch old movies…or go out to the lake and feed the ducks the rest of these waffles."

"Ducks?" Drew rolled his eyes. "We're not little kids."

"So then, how about feeding the ducks and then going on a hike?" Belatedly, Abby remembered Lily's weak left leg, from a club foot that hadn't been properly treated when she was in foster care. She thought up a fast excuse to avoid a long walk. "I'm too tired to walk very far, but we could follow Sapphire Lake and watch the Jet Skis and sailboats for a while."

Tyler and Drew exchanged bored looks that revealed just how exciting *that* sounded. Then Drew gave Tyler's shoulder a playful shove. Tyler bent to tackle him at the waist and they hit the floor, wrestling like a pile of puppies until Abby managed to call a halt.

"Monopoly? Scrabble?" Abby searched her memory for any games she'd liked at their ages, but without siblings or close friends, she'd spent most of her childhood between the pages of good books. "Cards?"

Drew dove in for a sneak attack on Tyler and they crashed against the sofa. It screeched against the hardwood floor.

"Stop!" she ordered. *"Now."*

Chastened, they fell apart, breathing hard—and then Tyler punched Drew in the ribs and they were at it again.

"Grab your shoes. We're leaving." She thought fast. "I could use your advice, really. Do you guys know anything about pets?"

That got their attention.

"Why?" Tyler asked, dodging another feint by Drew.

Hubert's broom handle began pounding an all too familiar rebuke.

"I, um, think I'll be moving very soon." *Maybe sooner than I planned.* "And I was thinking about checking out the animals at the shelter. Would you like to go there and help me look? We'll need to hurry, though. I think they close at eleven on Saturdays."

"Awesome!" Drew spun away and pulled his Nikes from the pile of shoes the kids had left at the door. "A big dog would be really cool. Like, a guard dog, or something."

"Something cuddly," Lily ventured, her

eyes downcast. "With big brown eyes and lots of white fur."

"Maybe a hedgehog." Tyler grabbed his own shoes and jammed his feet into them. "You could even keep it in your pocket when you were at work."

The image made Abby laugh out loud. "Interesting idea, sport. Now tell me how you'd get it *out* of your pocket!"

Given an interesting activity, the boys seemed to have forgotten their wrestling techniques. Abby breathed a sigh of relief. After an hour at the shelter and an hour or so at the lake, they could stop at that little malt shop in town for lunch.

With luck, she could find something else to entertain them until three, and then she could give them all back.

If she lasted that long.

How on earth did mothers survive day after day after day?

THE KIDS BOUNDED out of Abby's car when she pulled to a stop at the animal shelter. She rested her palms at the top of the steering wheel and dropped her head against them for a moment, still reeling after Hubert's announcement from his porch.

That's it. Your phone jangles day and night. You come and go twenty-four hours a day and create a ruckus. Be out of here when your month's rent is up July eighth. If you find another place sooner, I'll gladly refund the difference.

He'd stalked back into his house but, Hubertlike, didn't slam the door. He closed it quietly…with the finality of a judge passing sentence on a habitual felon.

She'd tried explaining the late-night calls from the hospital staff. The times she'd had to go back to the hospital for emergencies or to cover for a nurse who'd called in sick. The fact that the kids were just a one-time deal.

But to Hubert the explanations hadn't mattered.

If she hadn't been so aware of the stares of several neighbors watching from their porch swings and the curiosity of the three kids, she might have found it almost funny.

At a sharp rap on her car window she looked up to find three eager young faces plastered to the glass.

"Come on!" Drew urged. "They won't let kids in there without an adult!"

Hurry, Tyler mouthed, as if she couldn't hear through the door.

She got out of the car and took them into the shelter where the smell of pine disinfectant, dogs and cats assailed her nostrils.

An employee on the phone waved them on back. Down a short hall behind her, two rooms housed dogs and cats, and a third held a variety of small pets.

The boys headed straight for the door marked Dogs, while Lily veered off into the room at the left with a cat decal on the door.

Abby wavered, then bore to the right, figuring that the cats could scratch…but dogs had bigger teeth and she already knew the boys were impulsive.

Sure enough, Drew was on his knees in front of a giant black dog, his finger wiggling through the wire mesh. "Drew!"

He shot an unrepentant glance at her and went back to cajoling the dog to come closer.

"Drew," Abby repeated, touching his shoulder. "We have no idea about that dog's temperament. I want to give you back to your mother in one piece."

He reluctantly pulled his hand back. "This is a *really* cool dog."

Several cages down, Tyler had passed a pen of gamboling beagle mix puppies to crouch at a cage that appeared to be empty at first glance. "What did you find?"

He looked up at her, his eyes swimming with tears, then threaded his fingers through the mesh and whistled softly. "Here, boy. Come, on."

At the back of the cage, a medium-size dog had pressed itself as far into the corner as it could. Possibly a springer-golden retriever mix, Abby guessed, given its dingy gold-and-white-spotted coat and the freckles.

Drew's favorite glowed with good health, its coat and eyes gleaming. This poor fellow, with one bandaged leg, was covered in mats and burrs. His thin sides were heaving as if he'd just run a long way. Pneumonia, maybe?

"This is the saddest one here," Tyler whispered. "This is the one you should take. He *needs* you."

"He does look sad, but I can't choose one just yet." Abby rested her hands on Tyler's shoulders. "I need to find a new place to stay—and there aren't many options. I might not be able to find one that allows pets."

"That almost happened when we moved here. We had to get permission before we could keep our dog, Scout. Maybe you could ask?"

The dog in the corner lowered its head and painfully eased onto its belly to crawl forward a few inches. Its sad brown eyes were fastened on hers as it moved, and its timid approach drew her more than any of the bouncing, excited tail-wagging in the neighboring pens. "I wonder what happened to this one."

At the sound of footsteps, Abby turned to see the attendant coming down the aisle. "Stray. She's not doing too well, though."

"So it's a girl, then."

"Yep. Looks like she had puppies a couple months ago, but no one has seen any sign of them. Maybe the owner found homes for them and just dumped her off in the country."

Outrage burned Abby's stomach. "That's horrible."

"The jerk probably figured it was cheaper than paying to have her spayed." The middle-aged woman shrugged. "Happens all the time, and we end up with whatever survives. This one got hit. I'd guess she was out on some road, trying to follow her owner's car after he dumped her."

Abby's stomach churned. "Someone who didn't even care if she starved."

"She's still starving. Won't eat. Barely drinks. I'd guess she's homesick, in addition to her injuries."

Sure enough, full pans of food and water in the pen appeared to be untouched.

"But she'll find a good home, here. A second chance?"

The woman glanced briefly at Tyler, who was still staring at the dog. She shook her head. "People want young and healthy dogs. Outgoing, playful animals. This one's so scared and nervous, we haven't even been able to brush the knots out of her coat."

The dog stopped at the center of the cage and rested its chin on the concrete between its outstretched front paws.

The pain and sadness in its huge brown eyes seemed to wrap around Abby's heart. "I wish I could have a dog where I live now."

"Don't worry about it."

"I just moved here, but I'll be looking for

another place to live. Do you think she'll still be here at the end of the month?"

"There'll be other dogs. Young, healthy, low-maintenance dogs."

"And I work full-time, so a dog would be alone..."

"Then you should get a cat. Me? I prefer cats. No worries about letting them in and out."

"But..." The pager vibrated at her hip. Abby looked down at the text message and sighed. "Hey, guys, we've got to go."

"Aw, can't we stay longer?" Drew had ventured to the other side of the aisle, where he'd started fondling the silky ears of a cocker. "Please?"

"I've got to get to the hospital." Abby fingered the shoulder strap of her purse before meeting the woman's eyes. "How much time?"

"Time? Oh, you mean for Belle." The attendant lifted a page on the clipboard fastened to the front of the run. Her expression turned sympathetic. "Tomorrow, I'm afraid."

"If I paid..." Abby hesitated, then plunged ahead despite the warning bells in her head.

"Like a deposit, or something. Would that save her for a while?"

"We can't do layaways, ma'am. The manager says its strictly cash and carry."

"You can't hold her? For just a while?"

"People walk out and forget to come back, leaving us wondering what to do." The woman held out her hands, palms up. "We've had animals in limbo for months that way. Our budget is so tight we just can't afford it."

This clearly was not meant to be. Abby didn't have a home herself, much less one for the sad creature staring up at her. There'd be vet bills—maybe huge ones. And the pager at her hip was buzzing again, so she had to leave *now*.

"How much does adoption cost?" Abby said as she herded the boys toward the door.

"Eighty, with spay, worming and shots. But, ma'am—"

"What if I pay that, plus her daily board until I can take her? I'd give you my phone number and come back every day to check on her. Deal?" Abby spied Lily studying a canary in the Small Pets room and motioned for her. "But right now, I've got an emergency at the hospital and I've got to leave."

The woman frowned. "A rushed decision isn't always a good one. Come back tomorrow morning and I'll make sure she's still here. Okay?"

"Perfect." Abby handed her a business card, then followed the kids out the front door. "I'll be back!"

"THE DOCTOR will be here in just a moment, Mr. Matthews," murmured the E.R. nurse as she took his vitals.

Ethan winced and looked away when she lifted the edge of the blood-soaked bandage on his forearm. Keifer's voice filtered down the hallway from the receptionist's desk, where the woman had promised to keep an eye on him. "Where's my dad? I want to see my dad!"

An indistinct voice responded and his son quieted, but Ethan knew this ordeal had to be terrifying for him.

The boy's mother had just dropped him off last night for the summer, and at this very moment she was flying out of the country. And then on his very first morning here, the poor kid had seen his dad nearly lose an arm in the power-take-off mechanism of a grain auger.

The stuff of nightmares, surely, and the irony was almost as painful as Ethan's injury.

He'd wanted the next three months to be a wonderful adventure because he only saw his son for part of each summer and on alternating holidays.

From the lobby area, Ethan heard kids arguing over something. He frowned, remembering the icy blonde who'd walked into the hospital just ahead of him with her three children.

She'd breezed through the lobby with an offhand, "Keep an eye on these three, Beth!" And then she'd disappeared down the hall.

Some people, like his ex-wife and that presumptuous blonde, certainly showed little interest in motherhood, far as he could tell.

A woman in a white lab coat with a stethoscope draped around her neck hurried into the room. "I'm Dr. Jill Edwards," she said with a sympathetic smile. "I hear you had an argument with an auger."

"It won. The painkiller is really starting to kick in, though." Ethan rested his head against the paper-covered pillow on the gurney and regretted every moment of this day as Dr. Reynolds carefully unwrapped his haphazard bandaging.

She sucked in a sharp breath. "This is beyond the scope of a hospital this size, Mr. Matthews."

Startled, he looked up at her as she gently cleansed the edges of the wounds and then firmly wrapped the arm again with clean bandaging. She nodded to a nurse, who quickly shoved an IV stand next to the other side of the bed and opened a package of IV supplies.

He winced when she placed the IV needle in his arm. "It's only a few lacerations, right? You can sew them up?"

Dr. Edwards shook her head. "It's more involved than that. You've lost a lot of blood and you stand a good chance of losing function of your hand—or worse—if this isn't done right. I'm referring you to an excellent surgeon in Green Bay."

Ethan closed his eyes as the deadline he had to meet and the activities he'd planned for Keifer all went up in smoke. "That isn't necessary. Last year I needed thirty stitches when a bull took after me. Doc Olson stitched it up in his office and it healed good as new."

"The tendons and nerves are involved, and the wound is badly contaminated." The doctor nodded curtly to the nurse, who moved to an intercom on the wall and instructed someone to make arrangements for transport and admission to a hospital in Green Bay. "You need this taken care of as soon as possible."

"I...can't do it."

"Mr. *Matthews*—"

"*No.* I have my son with me for the summer. I don't have relatives here, and there's no one else to take care of him."

Removing her gloves, Dr. Reynolds murmured something to the nurse, then she turned back to him and lifted the rail on his gurney. "We're going to find someone to help you out, so don't worry."

"If...if I do go, that would just be an outpatient deal, right? Back here today?"

"Maybe. And perhaps you could come here for follow-up care."

"Follow-up?"

"If you should need IV antibiotics and dressing changes." She looked over her shoulder. "Ah, here you go. I need to check on someone else, but I'll be back in a few minutes."

Someone slipped into the exam room just out of Ethan's visual range and spoke quietly to the doctor, then moved to his bedside.

It was the blonde who'd, like the Queen of England, so casually dumped her kids on the overworked receptionist. "I'm Abby Cahill, the director of nursing. I understand there's a problem?"

He was starting to feel woozy, now that the pain meds were hitting his system, but he wasn't too out of it to catch her patronizing tone. "I just need to take care of this here and get home. In fact, I could probably just leave right now." He started to sit up, but she gently pushed him back down. "If I keep it bandaged—"

"Mr. Matthews!" She blew out an exasperated sigh. "I really don't believe you're thinking clearly right now. Do you realize how serious this is?"

First patronizing, now insulting. He felt his blood pressure kick up another notch. "I can't go to Green Bay. What about my son? Keifer must be terrified."

"Beth is entertaining him," Abby said quietly. "As for you, the helicopter should be here in fifteen minutes. When it arrives, you need to get on it."

The room began to spin. "You don't understand. He's only ten, and—"

"He'll be fine. I'm sure the hospital social worker can handle this."

He bristled at her nonchalance. "I—I will *not* pawn him off on a total stranger."

"Mr. Matthews—"

"This is…the first time I've had him for an entire summer. I don't know any child-care people. But—" he gripped the rails of the gurney as his stomach started to pitch "—that…doesn't mean I'll let him go with just anybody."

"Our social worker is *very* trustworthy. I'm sure she knows some good families—people who work here at the hospital, even." Abby nodded decisively and headed for the door. "We'll get Linda in here right now, and see what we can come up with."

Abby was back in five minutes with a bony, middle-aged woman who looked about as comforting as a truant officer. "This is Mrs. Groden."

Frowning, the woman stepped to his bed-side. "Our local foster families are full right now, but I'll certainly find a place for your son if you're admitted in Green Bay."

"Overnight? No way."

"Rest assured—"

"No! How assured will *Keifer* feel, with someone we've never even met?" He tried to shake off the nurse who'd started taking his blood pressure again, but she clucked impatiently and he gave in.

"All right, then," Abby said. "You've met me, at least. I can keep him for the rest of the day. Overnight, if need be."

Not on a bet. He'd already seen her in action with those rowdy kids of hers, and he wasn't impressed. "I think…you have your hands full."

She glanced impatiently at the clock. "I'll just be here for an hour or so, until we can bring in a nurse to cover second shift. Your son will be safe with me until you get back. Scout's honor."

"No." But his head was spinning in earnest now and his stomach was queasy. And both Ms. Iceberg and her skinny social worker were starting to look just a little like angels with fuzzy halos above their heads.

"I *am* a nurse, Mr. Matthews." Abby's

voice came from far away. "I'll care for him as if he was my own."

"I'd volunteer, but I'm on call all night." The doctor's voice floated by. "Abby's an old friend of our hospital administrator and has taught nursing for many years. I assure you, your son couldn't be in better hands."

Ethan swallowed hard, fighting the inevitable. Then reached out blindly with his good arm for the plastic basin on the metal table next to his gurney.

Abby was there in an instant, one arm supporting his shoulders, the basin in position, and murmuring some sort of comforting words that barely registered as he threw up.

Minutes passed before he could find his voice. And he knew, finally, that he had to give in when the doc took another look at his arm and shook her head.

There was no way he could drive home.

"The Life Flight copter is just a few minutes out, Mr. Matthews," Abby said. "We need to get you ready for transport."

"M-my keys." He fumbled at his side with his good hand and found the truck keys in his jeans' pocket. "Two miles...out of town. Right on the church road...ten, eleven miles to the old corn crib and north past the Peters place. K-Keifer…knows."

And then the light in the room faded and darkness enveloped him as he listened to the soft murmur of voices too distant to hear.

CHAPTER THREE

KEIFER KNOWS, Matthews had said as he'd awkwardly tossed Abby his set of keys.

The boy knew what? How to get home? Knew about something that had to be done?

His father had certainly had quite a reaction to the Demerol…first exhibiting drowsiness and dizziness, then signs of respiratory depression. Coupled with his nausea, he'd been one sick puppy.

During her years in nursing Abby had rarely seen that level of response.

And now Abby was facing his son—a boy masking his obvious fear and confusion with a veneer of arrogance—who really, really didn't think he wanted to go with her, *anywhere.*

Pale and slender with close-cropped strawberry-blond hair and a dusting of freckles over his upturned nose, she wanted to reassure him with a hug. Fat chance.

The difference between him and the rowdy Reynolds boys—who'd gone home with their mother an hour ago—was night and day. The Reynolds were exuberant, mischievous, with a penchant for noise and trouble. This boy sat glaring silently at her as if she planned to kidnap him and sell him into child slavery.

It wasn't a surprise, though. Keifer had only seen his dad for a few minutes before the helicopter left, and the man had been ghost-pale and too groggy to make any sense. That alone must have been scary.

"Honey, your dad just had a little reaction to the pain medicine," Abby said gently. "He needs to have those cuts fixed on his arm, and then he'll probably be back here tomorrow. If they want to keep him longer, I'll take you up there to see him, okay?"

Keifer didn't quite meet her eyes, and his mumbled response might have been a yes or no.

"In the meantime, I told your dad I'd take care of you. I'd been thinking that you could just come home with me, but he gave me directions to his place. Do we need to go there?"

Keifer's chin jerked up and he gave her a level, challenging stare. "Chores."

"Like, dogs maybe? Cats?" The boy didn't answer, but feeding and watering a few pets wouldn't be hard. She took Ethan's keys out of the pocket of her lab jacket. "What time of day does he do these chores?"

"All day."

"You mean, several times a day?" Abby looked up at the clock. "I imagine he took care of everything earlier this morning. We could go out now and get it done, then get back to town for a late supper."

That earned her a derisive glance, but at least the kid followed her out to her car. He surveyed the vehicle with a dubious expression before hiking a thumb toward a battered pickup with big, big tires and a hydraulic winch mounted on the grill. "You should take Dad's."

It looked huge. It probably had a standard transmission. And driving it, she suspected, would be like maneuvering a bulldozer. "My car will be fine. Hop in."

Keifer slumped in his seat, glued to the door and folded his arms over his chest. She finally gave up trying to engage him in conversation when she turned off the main high-way onto a loose gravel lane through stands of pine and hardwoods.

Heavy gray dust boiled up behind the car during the endless miles to the corn crib Ethan had mentioned…which, she hoped, was that small structure just ahead. Tipping drunkenly into a maple tree, it could have just been an old shed.

A dirt road veered off into the trees a dozen yards past the rickety building, but there were no street signs or mailboxes anywhere. In fact, she hadn't seen signs of life for the past five miles.

"Okay, sport," she said after stopping the car. "Is this where we turn?"

Keifer slumped lower in his seat. "Maybe."

"We've come the right way so far?"

He craned his neck to peer out the window and shrugged.

"You've never *been* here?" Surprised, she turned to look at him.

"It was dark when I got here last night," he said defensively. "And we were going the other direction this morning. I don't remem-ber from last year."

Last year? What kind of dad only saw his

son once a year? Her opinion of Ethan Matthews dropped. "That's okay. We'll figure it out." She drummed her fingernails on the steering wheel, considering. "What do you think—should we take a chance on this little road?"

"I guess. I just remember it was kinda muddy."

A description that fit the farm lane quite well from what she could see after they made the turn. Leaning forward to see ahead better, she negotiated the ruts and bumps of the first mile, then breathed a sigh of relief as the road started to climb.

The tumbledown house off to the left might be the Peters place Ethan had mentioned. And ahead...

"Is that it?" She pointed across a shallow valley to fenced pasture. Beyond that lay a collection of buildings nearly hidden by a grove of trees.

Keifer straightened in his seat to see over the dash. "There's Buddy, Dad's horse. The cows are prob'ly over the hill. And the goats—"

"The *goats?*"

"Three. They're probably in the garden."

"I'll bet your dad wants them in there," Abby said dryly.

"Not really, but he can't make them stay out," Keifer announced with relish, his mouth curved in a faint, smug smile. "They can get out of anything, he says. Baxter's *real* mean."

As she drove down the next slope, the mud grew deeper, grabbing at the tires and pulling the vehicle to one side. An ominous stretch of deeply rutted road lay between them and the Matthews place ahead.

She debated briefly, then gunned the motor and held the steering wheel in a death grip as the car shot forward. *Halfway there. Three quarters...*

The vehicle slowed as it sank deeper and deeper until it mired down with its wheels spinning uselessly and mud flying into the air behind them.

"Shoulda taken the truck," Keifer observed, darting an I-told-you-so look at her.

"We might still be all right. Don't worry just yet." Abby unbuckled her seat belt and opened her door. The car was buried to its frame. "Okay. Now we can worry."

The bright afternoon sunshine had gradually disappeared behind clouds during the past half hour. Her cell phone reception was nil—barely one bar.

And the only towing service in the area was back at Blackberry Hill, though she'd overheard a disgruntled nurse complain that the owner often quit early and went fishing.

And she was almost *sure* she'd seen a truck emblazoned with Mel's Towing ahead of her car as she'd driven out of town.

SOMEWHERE BETWEEN the car and the next dry stretch of road, Keifer lost a tennis shoe in the mud and Abby realized her taupe slacks and loafers were a total loss.

By the time she and the boy trudged up the last hill—which was much farther away than it had appeared from the other side—and reached the Matthewses' mailbox, thunder echoed through the dark sky and bolts of lightning shook the ground beneath their feet.

"Run, Keifer!" Abby shouted over the rising wind. "I've got a key for the house."

"Dad doesn't lock it anyway!" he shouted back to her.

Even minus a shoe, he raced up the long driveway and reached the house well before she did.

Soaked and shivering, she joined him on the covered porch and stared out at the deluge. "Well, this is certainly an adventure," she said, wishing she dared put a comforting arm around his thin shoulders. "But at least we got here, right?"

He must have sensed her thoughts, because he pointedly moved a few yards away. He looked down at his muddied sock and some of his tough-kid veneer slipped away. "Mom is gonna *kill* me when she hears about my shoe."

"Surely that won't be a big deal. Not when she hears the whole story, right?"

When he didn't answer, she grinned at him. "Anyway, you're here with your dad for the summer. I'm sure he'll get you another pair if we can't find it."

"I guess."

"I suppose we'd better go inside, don't you think? You can put on some dry clothes, and I'll call for a tow truck. Then you can tell me about the animals we should feed while we wait for help."

She followed Keifer to the end of the wrap-around porch, where a side door led into the kitchen. It felt strange walking into Ethan Matthews's house with him away.

Several bloodied towels still lay on the counter by the sink, a macabre reminder of Ethan's accident earlier in the day. She quickly filled the double sinks with cold water and put the towels in to soak while Keifer changed upstairs.

By the time he returned, she'd mopped up the rest of the evidence of Ethan's injury and had left a message for the towing service. "I should call the sheriff and let him know about the road hazard, too. I'd hate to have anyone rear-end my car in the dark."

"No one lives back here but Dad," Keifer said as he rummaged in the cookie jar on the counter.

Now, there was an eerie thought, with a storm rumbling overhead and the kitchen lights flickering. "No one?"

"The road dead-ends just over the hill, so no one ever comes out this far, Dad says. That's why I can ride his horse all over and he doesn't worry."

"Oh." Feeling a sudden chill, she rubbed her upper arms. "So he doesn't have any neighbors?"

"He doesn't *want* neighbors."

Well, that certainly fit her impression of the man. A stubborn recluse, who clearly resented any sort of interference from others—even with a serious injury to contend with. Abby suddenly felt very sorry for Keifer, who faced an entire summer in such isolation. "So...we're entirely alone, then."

"Yeah." Keifer didn't look too concerned. "Dad likes it because—"

He broke off suddenly as a fierce rumble of thunder shook the house. He hurried to the window. "Holy cow. The animals are loose!"

She went to look out the window, too. Her heart sank. There had to be four or five cows milling just beyond the chain-link-fenced perimeter of the yard.

Her heart sank even further when at least three goats and several muddy sheep wandered by. "Where are they supposed to be?" she said faintly. "And how on earth will we put them back?"

He looked up at her, his cocky bravado now gone and his eyes wide. "I think I know where they belong, but I don't know how to make them go there."

So in minutes those animals could be

spread to the four winds, and there'd be little hope of finding them. And who knew how many more of them were already gone?

Matthews had been groggy when he'd handed her his keys, but she'd seen the distrust in his eyes and it had rankled ever since. For some reason he'd instantly judged her as incompetent…but who was he to judge?

She sure as heck didn't want to prove him right.

"Wait a minute, I remember a pasture fence running along the road when we came up here, and lining both sides of the driveway. Wasn't there a gate down by the mailbox?"

Keifer shrugged.

"If the entire property is fenced, and I can pull the gate shut across the driveway, then the livestock can't escape. Right?"

"Maybe." He chewed his lower lip. "But I don't know anything about the other fences."

"At least I'd be doing *something* to help."

A gust of wind blasted the side of the house and rattled the gutters. A light tap-tap-tapping overhead rose to a deafening roar as hail battered the roof. Torrents of marble-size pellets bounced crazily off the driveway.

The livestock were clearly agitated as they

disappeared into the sheltering trees. Where, she hoped, they wouldn't find another way to leave.

"The moment this lets up I'm running down to close that gate. Stay here in the house. *Promise?*"

"You kidding? There's no way I'm going out there."

She waited until the hail stopped and the rain slowed, then grabbed a yellow slicker from a peg by the door. Outside, she crossed the yard and ran down the long, sloping lane. Slipping and sliding, she careened into a fence post once and then fell to her knees at the bottom of the hill.

With cold, wet fingers she struggled to untwist the wire that held the metal pipe gate securely open. She dragged its heavy weight shut across the rain-slick gravel just as the rain began to pick up again with a vengeance.

"Of course. Why not?" she muttered as she started back to the house, her head bowed against the wind. Nothing had been easy since she moved here, and now she and Keifer were stranded at this isolated place with no way to get back to town.

And then a long, dark shape materialized

not twenty feet ahead. Its form blended like watercolor into the early dusk and driving rain, but the piercing yellow eyes were unmistakable.

She took in a sharp breath and stumbled to a stop, the hair at the back of her neck prickling. Her senses sharpened with an elemental awareness of danger. The house was too far away. There was no place to hide. She could never outrun it. The wolf took a step closer…

CHAPTER FOUR

ABBY'S HEART LODGED in her throat and her knees threatened to buckle as she stared at the wolf.

It stared back. Silent. So perfectly still that it seemed more apparition than real, its gray coat melting into the rain.

Primal fear flooded her veins with adrenaline. She took a small step backward. Another.

The wolf lifted its head, its gaze never wavering.

But there was nowhere to run.

Behind her, past the gate, Keifer had told her there were thousands of acres of government land. Even if she could scramble over the wire fence, the wolf could clear it much faster.

And running away would immediately identify her as prey.

Visions of lurid newspaper headlines rushed

through her head as she took another step back. "Nursing Professor Killed by Rabid Wolf." "Stupid City Woman Killed While Roaming North Woods of Wisconsin."

Through the mist she heard the distant sound of Keifer calling her name. And suddenly the situation was far worse.

Did wolves kill for sport? If she didn't show up and the boy came looking for her, would he be killed, as well?

At that thought she ripped off her yellow slicker. Swinging it wildly in front of her, she yelled at the top of her lungs. "Stay in the house, Keifer. No matter what, stay in the house!"

After a long pause she heard, "Why? What's going on?"

The wolf turned its head toward the house. Took one more long searching look at her. And then it melted into the shadows, leaving behind a swirl of mist and the sound of her pulse hammering in her ears.

It could still be waiting. And *bears*. Weren't there lots of bears up here, too?

Taking a deep breath, she put a tentative foot forward, then another, singing at the top of her lungs and shaking her yellow slicker.

Rain plastered her hair to her neck, drizzled down her collar. She slipped once on the slick gravel, slamming her knee against the rough stones and almost crying out.

Except that might be an invitation to a predator.

Forcing herself to walk steadily, she made another ten yards. Twenty.

Imagined the hot breath of the wolf at her back.

Thirty yards.

She almost wept with relief when she reached the porch.

Inside the kitchen she slammed the door shut and locked it, then dropped the raincoat, shucked off her ruined shoes and sagged onto a settee doubled over her folded arms.

"W-was something out there?" Keifer chewed his lower lip, his eyes darting nervously toward the door.

"Everything's fine. Just...fine." Shaking from the cold and the rain, but most of all from her overwhelming relief, she dredged up a smile. Then realized that she'd be doing him no favors if she didn't tell the truth. "I saw a wolf."

His tension faded to boyish disdain. "They wouldn't come up by the house. Dad said so."

She studied the poor young child, who could someday end up a snack for something with very large teeth if he wasn't careful, and held back a curt reply. "Well, this one did. Maybe he was lost in the fog, but he saw me, and I sure saw him. We are *not* setting foot outside this house again tonight."

He rolled his eyes. "Human attacks are rare," he said, clearly reciting what he'd learned from his father. "We aren't their natural prey."

"If my wolf could get lost in the fog, he could also mistake you for one very large rabbit," she said dryly. "Maybe he's got dementia. We're locking every door and we're staying inside."

When Keifer just rolled his eyes again, she gave up. "I could use some dry clothes. Could you help me find something?

That seemed to throw him. "Uh, there's only Dad's stuff here. He just has sweatshirts and stuff."

"Show me where, okay?" The lights flickered. "But first we'd better find a flashlight…

candles and some matches, too. We might not have electricity much longer."

She glanced around the kitchen—a Spartan place, with bare windows, stark white cabinetry and none of the homey touches indicating a family lived here. On top of the cupboards she found a serviceable kerosene lamp and a quart of lamp oil.

Keifer pawed through the kitchen drawers and held up a box of matches and some white tapers. In another drawer, he found a flashlight.

"I think there's more candles in the living room. There's a fireplace, too."

She put the lamp and candles on the round oak kitchen table and followed him. "Any wood?"

"Uh-huh." Keifer switched on the light in the living room.

Close at his heels, she pulled to a stop.

Because the kitchen was devoid of personality and warmth, she'd expected the same in here. But this room, a good twenty by fifteen, was paneled in dark, burnished oak, with a lovely crystal chandelier hanging over a long dining room table. Beyond that, a matching set of overstuffed chairs, sofa and love seat were grouped in front of a massive stone fireplace, which took up half of the far wall.

With the framed Robert Bateman wildlife prints on the walls, Navajo throw rugs on the oak floor and gleaming brass-and-glass sculptures accenting the end tables, it was a comfortable and very masculine room. Right down to the dust, Abby thought with a smile, glancing again at the chandelier.

Keifer crossed the room to the fireplace and prodded a well-stocked kindling box with his foot. "He's got lots of logs, if we want a fire."

"That's a relief. You wouldn't by any chance be a Boy Scout, would you?"

His head jerked up. "Why?"

Touchy. What was it with this kid? "I just wondered if you knew how to start a fire, that's all."

Behind her, an open staircase with a log railing led to a balcony, where three doorways presumably led to bedrooms. To the left of the fireplace, a door stood ajar. She rubbed her upper arms, shivering. "I can take care of making the fire. But first, I need some dry clothes."

The boy put several logs in the fireplace.

Studied them, then arranged them in the reverse order. From the stubborn tilt of his chin she suspected that it was just guesswork.

"Um, Keifer, could you tell me where I'd find your dad's closet?"

The boy hitched a thumb toward the door near the fireplace.

"You don't think he'd mind if I borrowed something?"

"Nah. He always wears the same old stuff anyway."

Maybe this charming room was out of character, but Ethan's choice of clothing apparently wasn't. It really was surprising, she thought as she moved to the doorway and tentatively reached inside for a light switch. A recluse like Ethan, having such a lovely home.

Inheritance, maybe.

Or the lottery.

Perhaps even something illegal, which would account for his worry about a stranger taking care of his son. Kids tended to talk too much and if there was some sort of evidence…

She pushed the door open wider, expecting to see a sea of clothes scattered across the floor and a rumpled bed that hadn't been made since 1970.

But again, Ethan surprised her.

The bedroom was huge—easily double the size of her own back in Detroit. There was definitely male clutter. Magazines piled next to the bed. A pair of jeans and a shirt slung over a chair. But the log-framed bed was made, and intriguing wildlife paintings hung on the walls.

Filling the wide outward curve of floor-to-ceiling windows stood a built-in desk topped with a computer, two printers and a phone/fax. Stacks of paper tilted precariously on the desk, on the floor next to it and on the chair. There were books open on every flat surface not filled with electronics and crumpled wads of paper lay like snowballs across the hardwood floor.

Whatever Ethan Matthews did, he certainly did with a vengeance.

She stopped to study a framed eight-by-ten on the bedside table. Ethan sat on a boulder with the boy—perhaps four or five—on his knee. Fall sunshine lit a backdrop of bright fall leaves and caught the golden highlights in his chestnut hair.

Abby's breath caught at seeing the man in his element. She'd seen only his injury. His stubbornness. She'd been focused on his immediate need for appropriate care.

Here, his teeth flashed white against the tanned planes of his face. She couldn't help but appreciate his broad, muscular shoulders, square jaw and strong cheekbones, yet she was even more impressed by the protective way he held his son.

Standing in his most personal space, she suddenly felt very much like an intruder. "Hey, Keifer," she called over her shoulder. "Could you come here a second?"

He grudgingly showed up a few minutes later, a smudge of soot on his cheeks and his fingers blackened.

She hid a smile. "Could you help me find those clothes you mentioned? I hate to go hunting through your dad's things."

"The drawers," he mumbled, pointing across the room. "Over there."

She'd made it past the king-size bed when a loud *crack!* shook the house and the lights went out. The pungent, sharp tang of ozone filled the air.

She spun toward the door. Stumbling over

something, she reeled into the edge of the desk. A towering stack of paper showered to the floor. "Keifer! Are you all right?"

He didn't answer. *"Keifer?"*

Shuffling through the paper on the floor, she reached to steady herself against the desk and yet another stack of documents cascaded over the edge.

"Keifer!"

When she finally reached the door, the empty living room was dark and illuminated only by flashes of lightning, and she could hear the back door in the kitchen banging against the wall as gusts of damp air blasted through the house.

A door she'd locked just minutes ago.

"Oh, no," she whispered into the darkness. "Why would he leave?"

IGNORING THE SOUND of Abby calling his name, Keifer took a wary step off the porch stairs, clutching the edges of his rain slicker together with one hand. He aimed the flashlight around the yard, hoping Rufus would come running.

It was all the way dark now, with the rain falling in steady icy sheets. Such total blackness that the flashlight hardly mattered, and with the wind tearing at his raincoat, the beam wavered, creating spooky shapes and shadows.

Shaking as much from the cold rain as his lifelong fear of the dark, he took another step. And another. Then he gave up trying to hold the coat closed and gripped the flashlight with both hands. "R-Rufus? Roooo-fus!"

He heard whining from the direction of the toolshed. A faint yelp.

Lightning flashed. The surrounding trees lit up for a split second, their gnarled branches reaching for him, the whorls of bark on their trunks forming misshapen faces straight out of some slasher movie.

Stifling a sob, he ran to the shed and fumbled with the latch. From inside he heard the frantic scrabbling of toenails against the wood and a sharp bark. "Rufus?"

She burst through the door the second he got it open, twisting and wiggling around his legs, jumping up to lick his cheek. He fell flat on his butt, his hands palms down in the squishy mud. She licked his cheek again, but by the time he scrambled to his feet she'd disappeared into the shed again.

"Rufus!" He tried to fight back his panic as lightning struck again. "C'mon, girl. *Please!*"

She didn't appear.

Warily, Keifer aimed the flashlight into the shed. Creepy stuff hung from hooks: ropes and saws and garden tools, the glittering blade of a scythe he'd seen Dad use to cut weeds. A few old rabbit cages were piled in a corner.

In the center, an old quilt covered a lumpy shape roughly the size of a grizzly.

"R-Rufus?" he whispered. "Where are you?"

Thunder rumbled through the sky, shaking dust from the rafters. He wavered, took a step back.

The black lab emerged from the shadows a second later with something small and limp hanging from her mouth. His stomach lurched. A *rat?*

Then something clamped onto his shoulder, and all he could do was scream.

CHAPTER FIVE

KEIFER'S KNEES BUCKLED as he panicked. *Escape—but where?*

He was already too far into the shed.

The door was blocked—

"It's just me, honey...I called your name. Over and over." Abby released his shoulder and patted him on the back, talking loudly above the wind-driven rain lashing the shed. "You scared me to death, running off like that!"

His fear turned to embarrassment and anger. "You're not my mom."

"I'm responsible for keeping you safe," she said in an even voice. "Let's go into the h—"

She stared over his head. He turned and saw Rufus had returned with that rat-thing in her mouth. He suppressed a shudder.

"Did you know she was going to have puppies?" Abby crouched and crooned softly to the dog. "I wonder if your dad knew they were due?"

Rufus edged farther into the pool of light from his flashlight. Sure enough, she held a bedraggled pup in her mouth. "It looks dead," Keifer whispered.

Abby studied the puppy. "No, but I bet the poor thing is cold. Does the dog have a bed in here? Anything your dad might've set up to help keep her family warm?"

Keifer held out his hands, palms up. "He never said anything to me."

"I think I'd better check." Abby searched the floor with her flashlight.

Uneasy, Keifer looked over his shoulder at the darkness outside. *Anything* could be out there. Watching. Waiting. Back at home, he never slept without a night-light in his room and the hallway light on. Here, everything was darker. Lonelier. A lot more scary.

"Oh, dear," Abby called. "Two. Three. Four, five, six…I think there's seven, and they're all huddled together on an old burlap sack. I'll bet the mom wants to take them someplace else."

"The kitchen, maybe? We could make a bed there, and I could stay with them all night."

Abby didn't say anything for a moment, and he started to worry. "Are you still here?"

She reappeared with a small cardboard box filled with squirming puppies. Rufus whined and nosed through them, as if she was counting. "I was just thinking. You know, your dad's kitchen is awfully clean and tidy. I'm not sure he'd want dogs in there."

"Sure he would!"

"But I didn't see any dog dishes. I'll bet this gal is an outside dog, don't you think?"

"He has her inside, too, sometimes. Honest." Abby still looked doubtful. "Really. She's in the house *all* the time, and he just lets her outside a lot. I'm sure of it."

Rufus gently released the pup in her mouth. She licked it from head to tail, the puppy rolling over with each sweep of her tongue.

"Well...if you're sure." Abby frowned down at the pups in the box. They were shivering and squirming over each other as though trying to get warm. "Let's bring them in tonight, anyway. It's awfully chilly out here."

Rufus followed them anxiously to the house. When they reached the porch, Abby put the box down and held on to Rufus's collar. "You go on in and close the door to the living room, okay? And bring me an old towel so I can wipe the mom's feet."

In twenty minutes the pups and Rufus were settled into a corner of the kitchen in a big cardboard box cushioned with an old blanket Abby had found in the basement.

Keifer had found a sleeping bag upstairs and rolled it out next to the puppy's box. He'd brought in a stack of books, too. With the thunder rolling outside and the glow of light from the kerosene lantern on the kitchen table, it almost seemed like camping.

"I'm going to work on that fireplace," Abby said. "I think we'll want a little heat tonight… and the extra light would be nice. Maybe we can warm something up for supper, too. Like a campfire. Does your dad have any hot dogs? Marshmallows?"

Keifer hadn't seen *anything* in the bare refrigerator that looked as good as that, but he just shrugged and stared at the faint, muddy paw prints circling the kitchen.

Rufus had brushed up against the white cupboards, too.

He tried to imagine what Dad would say.

He sure didn't have to imagine Mom's response—she'd be totally freaked out. *Anything* involving dirt, animals, blood or sweat freaked her out. Which is why he'd never had any real pets. Only some dumb fish that couldn't do anything but swim in circles.

After Abby left the room he stretched out in his sleeping bag, propped his chin on his palms and listened to the tiny squeaks and squeals from the puppy box.

He'd counted the days until coming here, but the first morning had been scary. And now Dad wasn't even here and a stranger had taken his place.

But Abby said he'd probably be back tomorrow, and the puppies… He squirmed caterpillarlike in his sleeping bag until he could see over the top of the box and count them all over again.

The empty feeling in his chest eased as he watched Rufus lick and nudge her pups. Even if Dad wouldn't be able to do all the fun things he'd promised, there'd still be puppies to play with, and Keifer *wasn't* going to be homesick for Mom and all his friends back home.

He backhanded a hot tear before it had

a chance to fall. Nope, he wasn't going to miss them.

Not much at all.

AFTER A SLEEPLESS NIGHT on the sofa, Abby cracked an eye open to look at her wristwatch. She flopped back against the cushions and pulled the afghan up over her shoulders. *Five o'clock.*

When had she last been awake at five?

The storm had finally passed, but Rufus had barked anxiously at the door at least three times. She'd blearily shuffled out to the kitchen and then had stood on the chilly porch until the dog returned. Amazingly enough, Keifer had barely stirred.

Drifting and dreaming, only half awake, Abby snuggled deeper under the afghan, thankful for the marshmallow-soft sofa.

It was so peaceful here, the silence of the forest broken only by the distant hoot of an owl, a chorus of coyotes…gentle mooing.…

She sat bolt upright. *Mooing?*

Throwing back the afghan, she hurried barefoot across the cold hardwood floor to the window and squinted out at the gray predawn landscape. Heavy fog hung low to the ground, leaving the tops of fence posts and bushes hovering weightless several feet above the ground.

Farther away, large dark shapes drifted past like ungainly rowboats floating on a sea of fog. Very *oddly* shaped boats. One of them mooed.

Keifer pushed open the kitchen door and stood next to her, his hair tousled. "Weird," he observed after a loud yawn. "So, are you gonna do chores?"

Chores. Interesting concept, that. What, exactly, did chores entail? She rubbed her upper arms and considered. "I don't suppose your dad has a list?"

Keifer looked at her with the patience of a person dealing with the mentally incompetent. "He just does them. Why would he need a list?"

Lists were comforting. It was fun, making lists of things to do and crossing off each success. Without a list…on foreign ground… she was at a complete loss.

She crossed her arms and tapped her fingers on the bulky sleeves of the sweatshirt she'd borrowed. "If there's no list, have you *seen* him do chores? I assume those cows get food. And what about the horse and those goats you mentioned yesterday?"

"I don't know. I just got here." Keifer shrugged. "Their food's probably in the barn."

"I'm sure it is, but I don't know how much or what kind to give them." She had an unsettling thought. "Um, he doesn't *milk* those cows, does he?"

Keifer rolled his eyes. "They're the beef kind, but he doesn't eat them. He says, 'Anything that dies here, dies of old age.' He gave them all names."

"Names?"

"Yeah. He was gonna raise cattle for money, but then they all sorta got to be pets. So now he says they're the lawnmowers for his meadow."

Feeling more and more like Alice after she'd tumbled down the rabbit hole, Abby sighed. "So, this mowing crew of his, have you ever seen your dad feed them?"

Keifer shrugged.

"Maybe we'd better try contacting him. He probably had his arm fixed last night, and he might even be on his way home. If I can track him down, maybe he'll tell us what he wants done."

Far more confident now, she tousled Keifer's hair and went to the phone in the kitchen. In the far corner, Rufus raised her head over the box, then dropped back down, clearly occupied with her new family.

The line was dead.

Abby reached for her purse and rummaged for her cell phone. Her hope faded at the words *No Service.*

No way to contact the outside world.

No car—because hers was still mired in the road.

And, she remembered with a heavy heart, she'd promised to contact the animal shelter this morning about that poor dog on death row.

But *surely* the shelter wasn't open to the public on Sundays, anyway. And surely the staff scheduled to feed the animals wouldn't actually euthanize anything today…would they?

Biting her lower lip, she leaned against the kitchen counter and rubbed her face, the image of that sad, wary dog all too fresh in her mind. "I'm going outside, Keifer," she called. "Can you tell me where the barn is?"

He came to the doorway. "Past the house. Driveway goes back there."

Here, at least, was a ray of hope. She remembered driving through Wisconsin's dairy country and seeing herds of black-and-white diary cattle lining up to get into their barn. Did beef cows know that trick, too?

"Maybe the cows will, um, follow me if they think they'll be fed."

Keifer wandered into the kitchen with a sullen expression. "The TV doesn't work. Not the computer, either."

"The electricity's out. Maybe you'd like to just crawl into your sleeping bag and go back to sleep while I go outside. It's too early to be awake, anyway." When he glanced nervously at the curtainless kitchen windows, she added, "Rufus will be in here with you, so you'll be fine."

"Uh…maybe I better come along. Just in case."

She hid a smile as she went to the back door. "If you prefer. I'm sure you're more of an expert at all of this than I am."

She sorted through a pile of boots, found a small pair that had to be Keifer's and handed them over. The rest were size elevens. After considering her muddied shoes, still wet from last night, she took a pair of rubber work boots, found some ratty yellow gloves and stuffed one into each toe.

"These are going to look like clown shoes," she muttered, looking up at Keifer. "Promise you won't laugh?"

He nodded solemnly, though his mouth twitched.

The fog still hung low and heavy, tinged now with the faintest shade of rose. The cows had moved farther toward the road, where—luckily—she'd closed the gate last night.

"Do you ever see wildlife around here?" she asked casually as she followed Keifer down the lane toward the barn.

"'Possums. 'Coons. Deer. No wolves, though, if that's what you mean."

He stepped into a mud puddle with a splash and nearly fell, his arms flailing. "Whoa!" She steadied him.

She glanced around at the forest still shrouded in mist…where something rather large could hide.

"I think I saw a bear once," the boy continued, "but it was pretty far away. Dad sees wolves, but not this close, so I never saw one. Pictures, though. Dad takes lots of pictures."

"Pictures," she echoed, trying to imagine the man she'd met as a photographer. "Really."

The lane climbed a gentle hill and soon they were out of the ground fog. "For his book."

"Like a picture album?"

"No, a book about wolves."

She glanced at Keifer, but the boy kept trudging on with his attention on the ground in front of him. If the kid had said Ethan Matthews raised platypuses and giraffes, she couldn't have been more surprised. "He writes *books?*"

"Not kid books, though."

"Really." Maybe the boy had things a little confused. The man she'd met at the hospital had hardly seemed the erudite, professorial type.

Ahead, probably another twenty yards, the first slivers of sunlight picked out a wooden barn that must have been constructed recently, and beyond it, a fenced pasture and a much older barn weathered to pewter-gray.

On the south side of the new barn, a ten- or

twelve-foot pipe gate hung askew from just one hinge, its top bars bent.

"I think we've just discovered how your dad's livestock got out," Abby said, relieved. "He must've forgotten to chain the gate."

"Dad doesn't do stuff like that. He's real careful."

"Maybe when he got hurt out here, he couldn't get it fastened. Let's bring a bucket of grain from the barn and see if we can lure some of those animals back, okay?"

"I'll get it." Keifer ran through the gate and disappeared around the building. He returned a moment later, ducked into the barn and soon came out with a bucket of corn that was obviously a heavy load for a kid his size. Puffing, he set it down at her feet. "I think this is weird, though."

She caught the handle of the bucket in one hand and tested the weight of it, then started back down the lane. "What's weird?"

Keifer chewed at his lower lip. "The pens for the sheep and goats were open, too!"

Abby switched the heavy bucket to her other hand and flexed her tender fingers. She smiled down at him. "He was hurt, so he was probably in a hurry."

"No. I mean, he was—but I was out here with him when it happened. He never opened those other gates."

Abby paused. "You said goats were smart and hard to keep penned, so maybe they just played Houdini."

"Who?"

"Houdini was a guy who could escape from just about anything."

"No." Keifer's voice held an edge of fear. "It wasn't the goats. The locks were sawed off, Abby. Why would anyone do something like that?"

Abby eyed the muddy barnyard. "I'll take a look if we actually get any of the livestock back up here," she said. "Now, let's see if we can round up some critters."

Thirty minutes later Abby was hot, muddy and frustrated.

The sheep and cows were nowhere to be seen, but shaking a bucket of grain certainly attracted the goats. They charged toward her as if that grain were their last, desperate hope for survival, then shouldered one another out of the way and nearly knocked her off her feet.

She hurried to the barn, with three irate goats butting at the bucket, and her.

Headline: "Foolish Nurse Lures Angry Goat Mob With Grain—Trampled to Death." Or, "Woman Chased by Goats—Spends Two Weeks in a Pine Tree."

Both sounded entirely too plausible by the time she'd finally trapped them in their pen.

Keifer, who'd brought up the rear, eyed them warily as she poured part of the grain into a feeder and quickly slammed the gate shut again.

Leaning against the gate to catch her breath, she ran a hand wearily through her hair. "I've definitely lost my fondness for goats," she announced. "How about you?"

But Keifer wasn't paying attention. He'd squatted by the gate to study something and held up a long heavy chain and padlock. "See, I told you," he said.

She stared at the ruined padlock. Then turned slowly to scan the nearly impenetrable forest surrounding the little buildings on three sides.

Shadows seemed to coalesce, materialize, then slink away. Every boulder, every clump of undergrowth offered a place to hide.

Someone had cut that padlock after Ethan left. Someone who'd wanted to cause trouble. But why?

And the bigger question... *Where was that intruder now?*

She turned to Keifer and reached for his hand just as a much taller shape loomed out of the mist not twenty feet behind the boy.

She bit back a scream.

CHAPTER SIX

ETHAN SPUN AROUND, expecting to find a ten-foot bear looming over him or an angry moose, ready to charge.

"Dad!" Keifer started to run for him, then faltered to a stop. His face looked worried as he stared at the heavy white bandaging that covered Ethan's arm from elbow to fingers. *"Holy cow."*

Ethan gave his arm a rueful glance, then welcomed Keifer into a one-armed hug. "I'll be good as new before long."

He looked over the boy's head at Abby. "W-we weren't expecting you," she said, her voice faint. Splattered with mud from head to toe, she gripped a length of chain until her knuckles turned white.

"I wasn't expecting to see you two, either, since I didn't see my truck in the drive. Where'd you park it?"

"About your truck…"

There were dark circles under her eyes and she was clearly exhausted. He felt a pang of guilt. Though much of yesterday was foggy, he dimly remembered handing her his truck keys and mumbling something about chores. "I shouldn't have asked you to come out here. Especially not in this wea—"

Lightning struck somewhere close with an earsplitting *crack* followed by a long, ominous roll of thunder. Raindrops rippled the puddles of standing water at their feet, and then it began to fall in earnest.

"The goats are in," Abby said over the rising wind. "But I didn't…get…"

The *goats?* He shook his head, unable to hear her clearly. "Get back to the house!" he shouted. Keifer took off like a jackrabbit. Abby tried to yell something else, but he gestured and started down the hill, shielding his arm with the tail of his shirt. If the damned thing soaked through, he'd probably need to go back to the hospital again. A long drive. A waste of time.

Whatever she wanted to say would just have to wait.

Keifer was already there when Ethan reached the back door. "Uh…just so you know, there's a surprise, Dad. I mean, maybe not a surprise for you, but to us."

The kid looked worried about Ethan's reaction, for Pete's sake. "What, is the power off again?"

"That, too."

Not for the first time, Ethan wondered about the life Keifer led with his mother. There was strict, and then there was *too* strict.

"I'm sure everything's fine," Ethan said as he stepped inside. "I—"

Rufus bounded across the room from her makeshift bed, her tongue lolling and her tail wagging her entire back end. When he crouched to give her a two-handed rub behind both ears, she leaned into his touch, her eyes closed.

High-pitched squeals erupted from her bed—a chorus of voices he hadn't expected for another week. He held the dog's face in his hands. "Well, there, Roof. How big a family did you have?"

"Seven," Keifer said in a small voice. "I heard her barking outside. It was stormy last night, so I went to find her. She was locked in the shed."

Knowing how timid the boy was about the

dark, that search for Rufus had taken considerable courage. "How'd you get shut in there, old girl?" He gave her a final pat and clapped Keifer on the shoulder on his way over to see the pups. "I'm glad you brought her inside. I hadn't fixed up a bed for them in the shed yet." Keifer's words suddenly registered. "You two came all the way out here yesterday, too?"

"We stayed. *All* night."

Abby stepped inside and shucked off her boots. "I see you've met the new additions."

He hunkered next to Keifer and counted them, then lifted each one. "Four boys, three girls. Nice ones."

"Rufus sure thinks so. She seemed really worried when we carried them to the house, and she's barely left them alone since."

"I understand you two stayed overnight. I sure never meant for you to go to all this trouble."

"That was unintentional, though probably just as well." Abby waved a hand around the kitchen. "We had a few problems."

He straightened. "I'm sure everything's fine. I'm just thankful..." His voice trailed off as he glanced around the kitchen. There were muddy dog prints everywhere. There were also three cake pans on the floor and one on the counter catching water drops from damp spots on the ceiling. "Oh."

"It's not just here." She indicated the living room. "I've got two buckets by the door. Your phone and electricity have been out since yesterday."

The kitchen was in a single-story addition to a two-story farmhouse, added when the former owners decided to side the place with rustic half-logs. They'd taken more than a few shortcuts that weren't up to code, as he'd been discovering ever since he bought the place five years ago.

The roof had started leaking after a wild storm this spring, and topped a long list of repairs to deal with this summer—just one more thing that would have to go on the back burner until his arm healed.

"I'm really sorry for all your trouble. Not what you expected to be doing on a Saturday night, right?" He groaned, suddenly remembering seeing her with her three wild kids at the hospital. "Oh, God. What about your family? Your husband can't be too happy about this."

"Family?" She cocked her head as if mystified, then chuckled. "You must have seen me with Erin Reynolds's kids. Believe me, I'd be gray if those three were mine. I took them overnight as a favor, but I was sure ready to give them back."

Oblivious to the conversation above him, Keifer looked up at Ethan. "Can I name the pups?"

Ethan nodded. "I don't see why not. I'll bet you're better at it than me."

"Which leads me to ask, who named her Rufus?" Abby grinned. "Or was her gender ambiguous at the time?"

Keifer blushed. "I named her when I was little, 'cause of the way she barked. You know, *grrrr-roof.*"

"Perfect." Abby laughed, her smile lighting her face and transforming it from pleasant to downright beautiful. "I definitely think you should name all those pups."

She raised a brow at Ethan and tilted her head toward the living room, probably planning to give him what for, once they were out of earshot. Which, truthfully, he probably deserved. Taking a deep breath, Ethan followed her to the fireplace.

She frowned at his bandaged arm. "Dr. Edwards thought they'd keep you a few days."

"Nice idea, but I couldn't stay."

"You went AMA?"

He shrugged. "Against medical advice? I guess, but I'll be fine."

"And how on earth did you get back out here so early?"

"A handy deputy brought me most of the way—though some fool left a car blocking the road a half mile back, down by the creek."

"Really." Her eyes narrowed. "How inconvenient. For the person driving that car, too."

He winced. "It's yours? I was just going to ask if you'd seen the driver."

"I called for a tow truck before the phone went dead, but the place was closed. I'm hoping the guy listens to his messages, because there's no way I can get my car out on my own. It's buried to its axles."

"Which means my truck is…"

"Back at the hospital."

"Oh, no." He rubbed a hand over his face. "I should've called."

"But the phone's dead, so you couldn't have. Even if you'd tried."

His arm was starting to throb like crazy and

he still felt a little woozy. He dropped into the closest chair and leaned back, his eyes closed. "So now we're stranded, until I can get someone to bring my truck out."

"Except I have your truck keys here. Still, you're lucky I didn't try learning to drive a standard transmission last night." Her voice turned cool. "Count your blessings."

He'd already seen her bossy, take-charge side at the hospital, so her prickly side came as no surprise. The similarity between her and Barbara was chilling. "Believe me, I'm frustrated with myself, not you." He rolled his head against the cushion to look at her. "This whole mess is my fault."

She appeared mollified, but that wasn't really a surprise. Barbara always had to be right, too.

Abby moved closer to inspect his bandage. "So tell me about this arm. Did they do surgery last night?"

He nodded. "Should've been a simple outpatient deal, so I could leave right after recovery. But the docs figured there was too much contamination. They gave me some sort of antibiotic superdrug by IV."

"Surely not just a single dose!"

He curbed his impatience. "I insisted on leaving, but for the next ten days I have to go back to town every day for IV antibiotics and a new dressing. At least I can go to Blackberry Hill Memorial instead of Green Bay."

"How can you drive your standard transmission to get there?" She eyed him doubtfully. "Do you have anyone who can help out?"

"I'll manage." Though the surgeon had been adamant about not using that arm for at least four weeks while the nerves and tendons healed. And after that, he was supposed to have rehab.

In the meantime, he had work to do. Chores. Customers coming in two weeks for a fly-fishing trip…and a son who wouldn't be enjoying the kind of summer he deserved.

But Ethan would have to figure it out. He had no choice. "Thanks for taking care of my son, and for coming out here. I know I must've been a real jerk at the hospital, yet you went above and beyond the call."

Abby stared at him in obvious surprise. Oh, come on, he could be sociable, when his life wasn't going to pieces.

"I was glad to help out. Though I'm afraid we had some other problems besides puppies and a leaky roof." She worried her lower lip. "Keifer doesn't believe me, but I saw a huge wolf in your driveway."

"I've never found any wolf tracks near this place, but you might have seen a coyote. They look like wolves to most city folk."

"It *was* a wolf. It was big and long, with close-set yellow eyes, and it stared at me for a good minute before it turned away." She shuddered. "I think it was sizing me up for dinner."

He shrugged casually to allay her obvious fear. "If you were a deer, maybe. Did I hear you say something about the goats?"

Abby brushed her fingertips over a bronze statue of a wolf on an end table. "That, and just about everything else around here with four legs—you name it, and it was probably on the loose."

"I shouldn't have asked you to come out here. Just keeping Keifer with you in town was—what did you say?"

"None of this would've been a problem, if I'd known what chores to do—and if I had any animals to do them for. But when we got back, your cows, goats and sheep were roaming near the house."

He sighed heavily.

"It was stormy and getting dark when we arrived," she continued. "I got the gate closed down by the road and just prayed there were no other escape routes."

"That gate would keep them on my land, but the sheep and goat pen gates were chained and padlocked when I left yesterday. So was the gate to the cow pasture by the barn."

"If you didn't lock Rufus in the shed, why was she in there? And your gates didn't open by themselves. Those chains were *cut*. Who would come out here and do something like that?"

He kept his voice nonchalant. "Maybe just some kids...a high school prank."

But he knew that wasn't true. A lot of people in the county were angry. A lot still held a grudge. This was the most personal retaliation so far, but he knew there would be more.

It was just a matter of time.

ABBY MOPPED THE KITCHEN floor while Keifer and Ethan went to the shed to build a roomy dog bed with high sides, so the pups couldn't wiggle away.

"Very nice," she said after they'd each taken a handful of puppies to their new home. "What are your plans for these little guys?"

Keifer looked at his dad in alarm. "You'll keep 'em, right?"

Ethan propped the door partway open with a cement block so Rufus could come and go as she pleased. "I don't need a pack of dogs roaming out here. I'll probably keep one and find homes for the rest."

"Do you think Mom will let me have one? Could you ask her?"

"I'll ask, but I can't guarantee she'll say yes, Keif."

"But you'll talk to her?"

Ethan nodded, though his hesitance was clear. "You know my opinion doesn't carry much weight with your mom. She's the one who'd have to figure out arrangements when she travels."

"She has old Mrs. Murdock stay with me when she goes someplace," Keifer said stubbornly. "So I could still take care of a dog when she's gone. And she's gone a lot anyway, so she wouldn't have to put up with a dog much herself."

Ethan's eyes reflected deep regret as he looked down at the boy. "I'll talk to her. I promise."

"Yeah." Downcast, Keifer went back into the shed.

"I get the feeling her answer will be no," Abby ventured.

Ethan's expression darkened. "The last thing she'd want is the noise and mess of a dog."

Abby glanced nervously at her watch. "Speaking of dogs, does your cell phone work? I need to call the shelter."

"My cell has pretty good coverage out here." He unclipped the phone on his belt and tossed it to her. "Be my guest."

"Do you have a phone book I could use?"

"In the kitchen, but they'd be closed on Sunday morning."

"I certainly hope so." At Ethan's bemused expression, she added, "I was there with Erin's kids yesterday, and I sort of fell for a hard-luck case."

Ethan gave her an odd look. "You're adopting a dog?"

"I have to, or they'll put the poor thing down. I don't exactly have a place to keep her, though. I'm sort of in between homes myself."

"So I heard."

"How? I just found out yesterday."

"Deputy Krumvald is the guy who gave me a ride this morning." A flash of humor lit Ethan's eyes. "Apparently he was sent out on a disturbance call at the Bickham house yesterday. You weren't there when he arrived."

Dumbfounded, she stared at him. *A disturbance call?* Hubert was even crazier than she'd thought. "How on earth did the topic ever come up?"

"I told him you had Keifer, and I needed to pick him up. But I didn't know where you lived, and you weren't answering the cell phone number the hospital gave me. Krumvald remembered your name."

The heat of embarrassment crawled up the back of her neck. Two weeks here and the police already knew her. Who else had heard about Hubert's complaints?

"I didn't know where you lived, so the deputy took me to your place," Ethan continued. The fans of wrinkles at the corners of his eyes deepened, and she could see he was struggling to contain a grin. "The old guy was still fuming."

She stiffened. "Hubert has a real problem with noise."

"Apparently not when he makes it. He took one look at the deputy's car and came outside to rant about late nights and phone calls all night and hooligans disturbing the peace."

"Believe me, I'm more than ready to move out."

"You might want to get him calmed down first. He was babbling about you being a 'woman of ill-repute.'" Ethan held up his hands when she started to sputter. "His words, not mine."

She broke into helpless laughter. "There could not be a woman on this planet with a less exciting life than mine."

At the sound of a truck lumbering up the drive, Ethan launched out of his chair and strode to the window. "Looks like your tow truck is here."

Abby followed him out into the yard to meet the truck. Sure enough, the front of her mud-spattered car hung from its hoist.

A burley man in grease-stained coveralls climbed out.

"You Miz Cahill?" he asked around a cigarette dangling from the corner of his mouth. When she nodded, he shook his head and hiked a thumb toward her car. "I'm Sam, from Sam's Garage. I got your car outta the mud, but it won't do you no good. You musta hit a rock, 'cause there's a hole the size of Texas in the transmission pan."

"And that means…?"

"Fluid all leaked out. Looks to me like the transmission burned out, too."

She swallowed hard. "Can you translate that into dollars?"

He chewed on his cigarette for a moment. "If the tranny's gone, it'll be fifteen hundred, easy. Might be able to pull something off a junker at the salvage yard, but no telling if we can get a match."

Her heart sank. "And if you can't?"

"We have to order one. Could be a week, maybe longer. When the new tranny comes in, then we gotta fit the job into the schedule."

She dredged up a smile. "Is dropping it over the nearest cliff or setting it on fire an option?"

He snorted, her attempt at humor apparently going right over his head. "Tree huggers around here would love that. Nope, it's either here, the junkyard or my garage."

"To town, of course." Had she remembered to eat anything this morning? She suddenly felt faint, as the impact of the repair estimate hit her. "Can I hitch a ride back?"

"Yes, ma'am, if you're ready to head out right now. The missus expects me back in time for eleven o'clock church, she does."

"Yes—" She caught herself, remembering Ethan's dilemma. "Wait. I should stay and help round up the livestock."

"No. You'd better go while you can." Ethan wearily shoved a hand through his hair as he studied the cramped cab of the tow truck.

She followed his gaze. "But you need to go after your truck, and we can't all fit in there. I can come back out here and pick you up, once I have a loaner car."

"Nah, me and a buddy can bring your truck out." Sam scratched his chin and studied the gray sky with an avaricious gleam in his eyes. "For, say, sixty bucks."

Ethan barely flinched. Abby had to give

him credit for that, but it was surely an excessive amount. "Forty," she blurted.

Both men turned to stare at her.

"Since you've already got this tow and repair job," she added lamely, "seems like a deal to me."

Sam considered, spat, then hobbled back to his truck. "Get in, little lady. We've got a long drive back, and I still need to make this trip one more time." He chortled as he pulled open his door. "Seeing as how your *man* drives such a hard bargain."

CHAPTER SEVEN

"SHE'S STAYING up here for the summer, just like me. Only she doesn't have any place to live." His face somber, Keifer watched the tow truck disappear down the lane. He'd arrived in Wisconsin with a veneer of tough-kid bravado. Now he had the air of someone championing the downtrodden. "And now she doesn't have a car, either."

Ethan treasured the solitude of his home. The forest. The wolves he studied and the silent, peaceful trails he walked. *Alone.* Except this summer, he'd looked forward to plenty of quality time with Keifer, when he wasn't guiding fly fishermen or researching wolf behavior.

Having another person underfoot was the last thing he wanted.

After Barbara, he'd felt no particular drive to bring another woman into his life—too high maintenance. Not even on a temporary basis, because temporary all too often led to permanent, and Barbara's bitter, vengeful departure had cured him of any desire to risk that again.

Abby's take-charge attitude was an all too vivid reminder of that unfortunate episode in his life. But now his initial relief at her farewell felt more like guilt—even though he'd *seen* Abby's eagerness to accept that ride back to town. "She'll find a place in town, much closer to her job."

"But her car broke 'cause she came here to *help* us."

"It broke because she isn't used to driving on the bad country roads. She's a city girl, Keifer, way out of her element. I imagine she found this whole experience frightening."

But Keifer's logic was inescapable. She wouldn't have been on that rutted, muddy road at all, if it weren't for Ethan.

"And she wants to save a dog," Keifer persisted. "Do apartments let people keep dogs?"

"Some might," Ethan hedged, trying not to think about the restrictive clauses at most of them. From the heavy stand of trees behind the house he heard the faint sound of his sheep bleating. Thankful for the interruption, he started off in that direction. "We'd better go round up the girls, don't you think?"

Keifer stood his ground. "Abby used grain to catch the goats. That worked really good. Abby said—"

Ethan gritted his teeth and kept walking. "If we just move around behind them, they'll head back to the barn."

"But Abby said—"

"Come *on,* Keifer." The words came out a lot sharper than he'd intended, but his arm was aching and it was time for a couple of pain pills. And the thought of hearing that woman's name invoked a hundred times a day loomed like a threatening specter over the rest of the summer.

Over his shoulder, Ethan saw Keifer kick a rock into the weeds, then start to follow, his head bowed. "Hey, when we get the truck back, would you like to run into town?"

Keifer shrugged.

"I hear you lost a shoe in the mud. We could get you another pair, and maybe rent some movies or video games." That earned him another shrug, but also a flash of eye contact. *Progress.*

"And then we could see if Abby's okay.

What about the dog? Could we help take care of her dog for a while?"

"I don't know, Keifer. I'm sure she'd want to keep the dog with her, if she gets it. And I'll bet the hospital staff will help her find a place to stay."

Of course, this was the height of the tourist season. People booked accommodations a good six months in advance, according to the local paper.

His own two guest cabins were usually booked from June through September by sportsmen who came north for prime fishing. This summer he'd delayed the reservations until almost mid-July, though, to focus on his research.

The first parties would arrive in a few weeks, and had scheduled a number of outings with him as their fly-fishing guide.

Outings that were going to be a major challenge with miles of gauze bandaging protecting the sutures in his arm.

And Keifer…what would he do with Keifer then?

During the weekdays, Ethan was usually at home working at the computer, so that wasn't a problem. But evenings and weekends were when he usually took clients fishing, and later at night he often went out into the woods for his howl studies on the wolf pack.

He'd had a babysitter lined up for the summer, a local girl home from college. But last he'd heard, she and her girlfriends were backpacking in the Rockies, with no plans to come home anytime soon.

At the sounds of rustling ahead he motioned for Keifer to swing wider to the right. "Let's get behind them, Keif. Ready?"

He moved forward and sure enough the three "girls"—puffballs of creamy-white— were grazing just ahead. One of them—either Sylvie or Doris—raised her head and looked at him, then took off at a trot to the left. The other two bleated and promptly took a sharp right.

Keifer whooped and hollered as he crashed through brush, waving his arms. The two sheep in front of him split up and disappeared into the underbrush. He stared after them, then looked over at Ethan. "What now?"

Ethan sighed. "They'll hear each other and end up together, and next time, we'll try to be a little less intimidating. Okay? Let's round up the cows, and then go after the girls a little later."

If they weren't successful, there might not be three sheep left in the morning. The farm was on the southern border of the Lake Lunara wolf pack's range, and the fairy tales were true. Sheep were very easy prey.

An hour later, three sheep and all but one cow and her calf had been captured.

Keifer, muddy from head to foot, leaned against the barn and yawned. "Are we done yet?"

"You've been a great help, son. Why don't you go on back and start rinsing off that mud with the garden hose?"

He didn't need to ask twice.

Ethan followed him until he made it into the fenced yard. "I'll be back in ten, fifteen minutes," Ethan called. "Stay put."

Then he headed for a spot to the east he'd glimpsed through the trees, a small grassy knoll surrounded by pines.

A place he'd avoided while Keifer was at his heels.

Even before he reached it, the smell of blood and death assailed him. Powerful. Cloying. An agitated mother cow paced through the trees. Calling for her calf. Then she returned to the knoll, warily skirting something on the ground.

Ethan stopped and stared at the dark, sticky pool. Only a few tufts of hair and blood-soaked grass remained of what had been a pretty little heifer. Wolf kill, maybe. The carcass could've been dragged back to a den where the pack would share the feast.

But there was another possibility. One he didn't want to consider.

Other predators were in these woods—some far more cunning, far more dangerous than a pack of wolves.

He'd already seen the evidence.

ABBY CALLED the animal shelter four times on Sunday. Each time, after listening to the answering machine's litany of business hours, she left a message and her cell number.

Now at her desk first thing Monday morning, she held her breath and dialed one more time. An unfamiliar voice answered.

"I'm calling about a dog." She coiled the telephone cord around her finger, her stomach tightening. "I came in on Saturday and left my name."

There was a long pause and the sound of papers shuffling. "I don't see any notes here, Miss—?"

"Cahill. Abby Cahill. I talked to the attendant around noon Saturday about this dog… it looked ill. Sort of frightened. I think it was a springer-retriever mix, and the attendant called the dog Belle."

There was a long sigh from the other end of the line. "That dog was scheduled for yesterday, ma'am. She was put down. We don't have much luck placing dogs like her, so we don't keep them very long."

Abby closed her eyes. "The attendant said she would save the dog for me. She *promised.* I tried calling yesterday, but no one answered. Are you *sure?*"

"We've got several vets in the county who volunteer for us. Sunday is when most of them can donate their time. I'm sorry, but the policies here are strict. We barely make ends meet for utilities and feed, month by month. Mostly, we're in the red."

"But—"

"Rae should have explained the regulations here, which are set by the county board."

"She did, but I had car problems and couldn't make it."

"We've got a lot of other dogs, some also running short of time, if you'd like to take a look."

"No, I…" The image of Belle's haunted expression made Abby's eyes burn. "I'll send a donation, anyway."

She cradled the receiver and dropped her head into her hands. One look into that dog's mournful eyes had made it clear the poor thing had had a miserable life. Where was the justice?

"Can I talk to you a minute?"

Abby looked up and found Gwen Iverson standing at her door. The stocky, middle-aged nurse had been an employee of the hospital for twenty years, and had been the day charge nurse in the long-term-care unit for the past ten. "Of course."

Gwen settled into a chair facing Abby's desk, her jaw set and her eyes flashing fire and indignation at odds with the puppy print of her pull-over hospital smock. "I know the hospital is trying to expand its services. I understand the reasons. But Dr. Peters has canceled his clinic appointments for the *second* time. I've already told Mrs. Reynolds, but I thought you should know, too."

According to Grace, the cardiologist from Green Bay had started offering appointments at Blackberry Hill back in April, and came on the third Monday afternoon of every month. The system was a perfect way for local patients to see a specialist without commuting to a larger city. But the system didn't always work. "Did he have an emergency surgery?"

"His office didn't say. Carl and I had to reschedule fifteen patients. Some of them are from outlying areas and we haven't been able to reach them, so they might already be on their way. Carl is *livid.*"

Gwen looked pretty livid herself. Abby tapped the eraser of her pencil on the desk. "Do you have any suggestions?"

"Using a cardiology practice with several docs willing to rotate here, so they always have a backup. More notice before cancelations. Finding someone who will make us a priority instead of an afterthought."

"Excellent ideas." Abby flipped the pages of her day planner and jotted a note. "Erin and I meet with the local doctors every Thursday morning at Ollie's Diner, and I'll make sure this is discussed." She looked back up at Gwen. "Anything else?"

"A young gal stopped at the nurse's station this morning. She said she'd just been hired, and came in for her TB tine and drug screening. I sent her to the lab, and Madge has her watching orientation videos."

"Good. Once Joan's labs are clear, I'll have her work with you for a few days, then she can shadow Marcia. The sooner we start scheduling her, the better, but we still need to hire two more."

"Thank goodness," Gwen said fervently. "Too many of us have been pulling double shifts this month, and over the summer most of us want to take our vacation time. I haven't even had time to walk my dogs this week."

"Losing three nurses this spring really hit us hard. I understand the hospital is advertising, but there just aren't many spare nurses right now."

"Or they don't want to make the move north for our pay scale."

Abby sighed. "That, too, though the board is aware of the problem and working hard to correct it."

"Glad to hear it." Gwen glanced at her

watch. "I need to get back out on the floor, but if there's anything I can do to help, just say the word. I heard you're looking for a new place to live."

"You're the second person who's brought that up," Abby said dryly. "Word does get around in this town. *Fast.*"

Gwen shrugged. "Deputy Krumvald mentioned it after church yesterday, in case I might know of some good places. I'm afraid I don't."

"Even if I have to drive from a neighboring town, it'll only be until late August." But at the doubt in Gwen's eyes, her confidence faded.

"I'll do some checking," Gwen assured her as she started for the door. "Around here, everyone knows just about everyone else, so I'm sure we'll come up with something."

"Thanks." Abby smiled, then bent over the staff schedules on her desk.

The scheduling process had given her a headache as soon as she'd walked in the door this morning. Tricky, managing coverage of three daily shifts for both the hospital and long-term-care unit when there weren't enough nurses to go around. It was—

"Hi!"

She looked up, surprised and delighted to see Keifer standing at the door. "Hey, stranger. What brings you here so early on a Monday?"

"Dad. He's just down the hall, getting stuck with a needle. That was too gross so I came to see you. The nurse showed me where to go."

"How's he doing?"

Keifer frowned. "He didn't feel so good this morning. He was shaking a lot and he looked sorta sweaty, like he had a fever."

"Really."

"We caught all the animals though. We had to chase the cows all through the woods, and the sheep, too." Keifer grinned. "It was pretty cool."

But all that stress had probably been hard on Ethan, who'd just had surgery and would have been far better off if he'd been able to rest quietly.

"Is your dad seeing the doctor today?"

Keifer shrugged.

"Did he tell the nurse he wasn't feeling well this morning?"

The boy lifted a shoulder again.

Men. "Let's go see how your dad is doing, okay?"

Down in the E.R., she could hear Dr. Edwards's stern tone before they reached the outpatient treatment room. Abby steered Keifer to the waiting area near the nurses' station, then followed Jill's voice.

An empty bag hung on an IV pole next to the exam table where Ethan sat fully dressed. His shirtsleeves were both rolled back to his elbows, revealing a heavy bandage on one arm and a cotton ball and Band-Aid on the other where he'd just had his IV withdrawn.

"Really, Mr. Matthews. We're going to have to admit you if this happens again." Jill finished wrapping his arm.

"That isn't possible," he said. "I'll...just try to take better care of this thing."

Jill looked over her shoulder at Abby. "Your friend came in running a fever, his dressing soaked and muddy. A couple of sutures had pulled free, too."

"It rained," he said wearily. "The livestock got loose."

Abby felt a pang of guilt over leaving him on Sunday. "I should have stayed to help you round up your animals. I'm sorry."

"But even now, are you going to be able to manage?" Jill shook her head. "Your incision has barely begun to heal. I've started a different antibiotic, but you need to take it easy for a few weeks…and make *sure* you get back here without fail for your IV meds and dressing changes. I'd much prefer admitting you for a couple days."

"No."

"Can you get someone to stay with you?"

He glowered at her. "That's not necessary."

"Even cooking and washing dishes will be difficult until this bandage is off."

"I can manage. Are we done now?"

"Until tomorrow." Jill jotted a note on his chart. "But if you start to run a fever again or the pain increases before then, call my office or this E.R., pronto. None of this I'm-tough-I-can-handle-it stuff. I know you don't want any additional surgery, and you sure don't want an infection that'll force you into the hospital."

He nodded as he stood and awkwardly rolled his shirtsleeves down. "Thanks, Doc."

"Keifer's out in the waiting area," Abby said. "He's worried about you."

"He needn't be. Thanks again for taking

care of him, though." With a nod, he walked out of the room.

Jill waited a moment to make sure he was out of sight, then grinned. "So how did it go?"

"With Keifer? He's a good kid, but I'm not cut out for this parenthood stuff. Give me a sick child and I do fine. For anything longer—I'm at a loss."

"I meant with his dad. That's one very handsome guy."

"If you like tall, dark and stubborn. I don't know who was more relieved when I left on Sunday—me or him."

"So you aren't going to volunteer to help him out again?" Jill teased. "Just so you can get to know him better?"

"Did you hear what he said? He doesn't *want* anyone to help him. He's a loner, and a grumpy one at that. Believe me, if I was actually looking, he's the last man I'd choose."

WHEN SHE RETURNED home Sunday, Crazy Hubert had come out onto his front porch to remind her that she'd been evicted, just in case she'd forgotten. As if. And this morning, he'd glared at her through his curtains when she'd left for work.

Of all the landlords in this town, she'd certainly found a dandy.

Her heart lifted when her phone rang. *Good news. This has to be good news.*

"I'm, uh, sorry to bother you." Beth, the hospital's young receptionist, cleared her throat. "There's…someone here to see you. She says it's, like, an emergency, but she won't give her name."

Mystified, Abby drummed her fingers on her desk. A person with a health emergency would have gone to the E.R. So far she'd hadn't had to deal with any disgruntled patients or angry family members, but a public place would be safer than the privacy of her office. "I'll be there in a moment."

Locking her door behind her, she hurried to the lobby. Beth sat at the reception desk and nodded toward a woman who stood looking out the windows.

Abby fixed a welcoming smile on her face as she approached. "Can I help you?"

"I hope so," the woman whispered. She turned, her hands knotted. It was Rae, the attendant from the animal shelter. The one who'd let Belle die. "Can you come outside for a minute?"

Abby hesitated, then followed her out the front door. The woman glanced around before walking to a cluster of bushes at the corner of the building.

Belle lay cowering beneath them, tied to a branch with a piece of twine.

"I—I knew you wanted Belle, but you didn't call or come on Sunday like you said. I told the vet about you, though. He said he just couldn't put Belle down if she had a chance for a good home—even if we didn't have the paperwork done. He said you could make a donation to cover the usual adoption fee."

Overwhelmed, Abby felt her eyes burn. "What a nice man."

"He said he'd clear it with my boss on Monday, but I begged him not to." Rae swallowed hard. "Thing is, she makes us follow all the county regulations to the letter. New owners have to be interviewed. Then there's a contract, and pet-care videos everyone has to watch. I saved another dog once and gave it away, and she nearly fired me. She said it was like stealing. So this time…"

"You could get fired?"

Casting a quick glance over her shoulder, Rae nodded. "I've got a baby, so I really need my job." Her voice broke. "If you don't take Belle, I don't know what I'll do. I sure can't take her back…since she was supposed to be euthanized."

Abby crouched next to the fearful dog and offered her hand. Belle belly-crawled a few inches forward to sniff her fingertips.

Hubert would never let her bring a dog into his house. Not even on a temporary basis.

She had no other place to live.

But this caring girl had risked everything to save this dog, at Abby's request. How could she refuse? "I'll take her. But do you know of any place that could keep her for just a while? A day or two?"

"I snuck her into my apartment last night, but no dogs are allowed. I could get evicted if someone heard her bark. And right now I gotta get to work." She reached into her pocket and pulled out a small tube of some sort of cream. "The vet gave me this for her sores."

"One last question—any ideas on where Belle and I can find a place to live?"

CHAPTER EIGHT

SHE'D FIGURED SHE HAD a few days to find a new place. Now, with a bedraggled and frightened dog sitting next to her in the shabby loaner car from the garage, she had a much more immediate deadline.

Hubert's bold No Pets sign tacked inside the door upstairs made his views on the subject all too clear. And Belle's rough appearance—which promised fleas and any number of doggy diseases—would worry even a dog-loving property owner.

Spying a small building with a Blackberry Hill Vet Clinic sign out front and Della's Doggy Boutique next door on the corner of Fourth and Elm, Abby circled the block and pulled into the gravel parking lot between the two buildings.

The receptionist inside the vet clinic gave Belle a dubious once-over, then took in Abby's crisp linen suit and matching heels with a narrowed look, obviously consigning her to the lowest dregs of society for mistreating a dog so badly. "Can I help you?"

Abby peered at the woman's name badge, praying a personal entreaty would help. "Hi... Yvonne. I was given this dog today, and she desperately needs an exam, shots—whatever you do. Is there any chance she could be seen today?"

The woman's accusing expression cleared. "Dr. Foster won't be back until three, and then she's booked solid until six. We might be able to fit you in before her appointments start, though."

In the meantime, Belle would have to ride around in Abby's car. Travel seemed to make her nervous, and right now she'd provide an all too vivid image of neglect that might alienate a potential landlord. "What about the grooming place next door," Abby said in a rush. "Do you recommend them? Perhaps she could have a bath and a flea dip there?" *Time—I just need a few hours of time.*

Yvonne smiled. "Della is Dr. Foster's aunt, and she's quite an animal lover. Let me call her for you."

Abby fought the urge to bite her fingernails

as the woman dialed then launched into a long conversation that appeared to cover every last bit of local gossip from the past five years. Belle whined and edged closer until she sat plastered against Abby's leg, clearly sensing that something was up.

"She can," Yvonne announced as she hung up. "She had a cancelation this morning. You could leave your dog and pick her up in a couple hours."

A couple hours. Abby bit her lower lip. "Do you board dogs here? I'm house hunting today, and I'm not sure what I'll find."

Yvonne shook her head. "We have a handful of runs, but we're full. Sorry."

"Anything else in town?"

"There was Rowley's, a private facility outside town." She frowned. "But that awful place was shut down last winter."

"What if…" Abby said a quick, silent prayer "…I take Belle over to Della's and leave my credit card number with you. Then, if I can't get back right at three, the doctor could do the exam and whatever else is needed? I'd leave my cell phone number, of course."

"Not a problem." Yvonne went to the desk

and quoted an approximate fee for the exam, labs and vaccinations and took down Abby's credit card number. "Just be back here by six sharp at the very latest."

Abby suppressed the impulse to kiss her feet. "You can bet on it."

IF YVONNE HAD BEEN perturbed by Belle's appearance, her reaction didn't hold a candle to Della's outrage at the obvious mistreatment the dog had suffered.

The woman was nearly as wide as she was tall, but she fluttered this way and that, fingering the dog's unkempt coat.

She muttered under her breath when she found wads of hair tangled at the base of Belle's ears, and darted an anguished glance at Abby when she discovered open sores beneath several of the biggest mats of hair. "This poor, poor baby!"

For all her wariness, Belle seemed to soak up the attention, and even licked the woman's plump hand.

"She's a beauty," Della said at last. "You won't see it today, but she's a fine dog. And if I could find the person who did this to her, I'd grab my shotgun and let him have what-for."

Relieved that the dog was in loving hands, Abby wrote out a check and hurried back to her car. There had to be an empty apartment somewhere in a town this size—or perhaps nearby.

She got the map from the glovebox and unfolded it on the hood of her car, then found a small notebook in her purse. She'd simply make a list of every neighboring town, and drive until she found something.

The weight lifted from her shoulders as she began to write.

ETHAN AWKWARDLY LIFTED the last sack of groceries into the back of his pickup and nearly fell over from the pain. The docs in Green Bay had warned him about taking it easy.

He hadn't realized how right they'd been until he'd gotten behind the wheel of his truck this morning to drive to the hospital. Just climbing up into the cab had been tricky without his right arm. Releasing the hand brake and shifting gears had been a nightmare.

And now he needed to figure out something for supper, do chores and get back to his computer…before his evening trek out into the woods.

Ethan settled behind the wheel, pulled his door shut and managed to fasten his seat belt one-handed on the third try.

"You should call Abby," Keifer said for at least the fifteenth time today. "She could help."

"She has a full-time job in town and we're a good forty-five minutes out."

"She could drive back and forth."

"Abby certainly seemed eager to leave yesterday, so I doubt very much she'd want to come back. And she'd be gone all day, anyway. So how much help would that be?"

"In the daytime, I could go along if you had to go fishing."

"But—"

"I'd be real quiet. Honest." Keifer's voice rose. "And what about all the times you need to study the wolves at night? Or early in the morning? If Abby was here, then she could stay with me. You can't just leave me alone!"

Arguing with his persistent ten-year-old son was eerily similar to arguing with his ex-wife. "I certainly won't leave you alone. I've put an ad in the newspaper for someone to stay with you. And I don't just 'go fishing.' I work as a fly-fishing *guide* in the summer. The guys I take pay a great deal for that service."

"Why look for someone else, when we could have Abby?"

"Drop it, Keif." Instantly regretting his sharp tone, Ethan reached for his cell phone. "I'll call home to check my answering machine. I'll bet someone has already answered my ad, anyway."

The ad—"fun, adventuresome college student for part-time summer child care"—had come out in Sunday's paper. So far he'd gotten three calls: a semi-literate woman who wanted to know how old the "kid" was and if he knew how to behave; a fragile-sounding grandma-type who didn't drive; and a college student who sounded as if he was high.

The only messages on the machine now were from his editor in New York and Keifer's mother, who'd breezily announced that she'd settled into her hotel room and would probably be too busy to call again for the next few days.

"So?" Keifer asked. "Any good news?"

Only that your mom is too busy to bother

talking to you. It wasn't any surprise, but it still irritated him. Barbara's career meant everything…and he'd caught a glimpse of that same attitude in Abby, even if she'd been a good sport about coming out to his farm.

Maybe the similarity between Abby and his mother made Keifer comfortable, and that's why he kept defending her.

"Your mom called. She'll call again in a few days."

"Oh." Expressionless, Keifer hoisted one ankle across the opposite thigh and picked at the trim on the Nikes they'd just bought.

"I know she wants to talk to you. Hey, maybe you could email her."

Keifer shrugged and looked out his window as Ethan wrestled the truck into first gear. "I want to go home."

"That's where we're headed."

"No, I mean I want to go *home.*"

"You know that's not possible. Your mom's out of the country." Ethan glanced over and saw a tear trickle down the boy's cheek. "But we're going to make this work, okay? And you'll be back with her by mid-August."

Keifer hunched closer to the door.

Just three days and I'm already a failure.

Guilt settled over Ethan as he drove. He'd promised the boy an exciting summer.

If Abby could make Keifer happy, then maybe it was time to contact her despite every inner warning telling him it would be a big, big mistake.

"I could give Abby a call," he said cautiously. "Though I'm sure she's made other arrangements."

"Maybe not."

"She won't want to commute that far."

"It isn't *that* far." Keifer twisted in his seat to face Ethan. "You won't even try to talk her into it, 'cause Mom says you never do anything *you* don't want to do."

Ouch. "Well, I can't make Abby agree. All I can do is ask." *And hope she says no.* "Deal?"

Keifer picked up the cell phone and held it out.

With a long, drawn-out sigh, Ethan pulled the truck to the side of the road and awkwardly reached over to fish through the glove box for Abby's cell number.

He punched it in on his phone. "But don't get your hopes up too high, son. Because I really don't think this will work out."

ABBY RESOLUTELY climbed out of her car and started for the motel office. The owner leered at her through the open doorway as she approached. "So, you decided to stay here after all?"

It was five-thirty.

The vet clinic closed in thirty minutes.

"I guess so." From inside her purse came the sound of her cell phone's musical ring.

Despite the fact that this guy smelled of beer and desperation, the shabby motel—a town away from Blackberry Hill—was the only place she had found that allowed dogs.

"You got the deposit?"

"Am I going to get it back? Those carpets aren't in the best shape as it is."

He drew back, clearly offended. "If the rooms here aren't good enough, you can go somewhere else, lady."

Which would be a park bench, if she didn't take this place right now. "They're fine," she muttered through clenched teeth. "Just give me the registration. I've got to get back to Blackberry Hill by six."

Her phone stopped ringing. Then its persistent, escalating ring started up again.

He opened a drawer, shuffled through

papers and pulled out a registration form and a ballpoint with the cap end chewed off. "Be my guest." He eyed her ringing purse with disgust. "Can't you answer that thing?"

Impatient to get back on the road, she jerked it out of her purse and glanced at the Caller ID. Ethan Matthews?

Eyeing the clock on the wall above the motel guy's head, she huffed out an impatient breath and answered it.

"Look, I know you aren't interested," Ethan said immediately.

In the background, she could hear Keifer groan. "Is everything all right? Is your son okay?"

"Fine. Everything is *fine*." Oddly enough, he sounded as impatient and edgy as she felt right now, watching the seconds tick by on that fly-specked clock on the wall. "I know we're a good forty-five minutes out of town, but Keifer tells me you don't have a place to live right now. He…er, we've got a deal for you."

The man across the counter shoved the registration form under her upraised pen. "Lady, I gotta get busy here. You staying, or not?"

Abby waved at him to stay quiet so she could hear Ethan.

"I'm a little laid up right now, but I need to be out several nights a week, at least, and it usually ends up being too late to bring Keifer along. What do you say—room and board in exchange for a couple months of help?"

At a sudden image of that rambling house, piles of dishes and scullery duty, she started to fill in the motel registration form. "I don't think so. I've just found a very nice place to stay."

"I figured as much. No problem."

In the background, she heard Keifer urgently saying something to his dad.

"Uh…we don't expect much. Just having an adult here when I'm gone would be a great help. Maybe you could share some of the cooking and help with a few odds and ends, now and then."

The guy behind the motel desk scratched the stubble on his cheek and *winked* at her. Revulsion pooled in the pit of her stomach. "You do understand that I work full-time?"

"Understood."

"And that I'm not a maid? I wouldn't be

doing housework. And, honestly, I'm not a very good cook."

Ethan sighed. "Understood."

"And you know I'm leaving Wisconsin the last week of August?"

"You've already made it pretty clear. But that's fine, because I only need help for the summer."

"I have a dog."

"And I've got hundreds of acres out here. That shouldn't be a problem."

"And…" She paused delicately, thinking of that remote, lonely place, without a neighbor for miles, and the fact that he was a strikingly attractive man who'd probably had women falling at his feet since he hit puberty. Not, of course, that she was that sort of woman. "Just to make things clear, I'm not looking for any sort of relationship."

He coughed sharply. "Believe me, you'd be *perfectly* safe."

The hint of laughter in his voice might have been insulting under other circumstances— like, from someone she was actually attracted to—but in this case it reassured her more than any number of words could have. "Then, Mr. Matthews, I believe we have a deal."

CHAPTER NINE

ETHAN FOUND IT AMUSING that Abby had carefully made it clear she was not interested in him while setting the terms of their bargain. She certainly shouldn't have wasted a minute worrying. Ethan had no plans to complicate his life.

Especially with a controlling, opinionated city girl given to lecturing him about his medical care at every turn.

Keifer, for all his insistence on offering Abby a place to stay, was nowhere to be seen, so Ethan stood alone on the edge of the porch and watched her pull up in a beat-up Chevy that had to be a loner from Sam's Garage. He felt a pang of remorse.

If not for him, she'd still be driving a decent car. She'd have taken that nice motel room in town. And, certainly, her own life would be less complicated.

Abby stepped out of the car in a rumpled

yellow suit the color of a highway Yield sign, her hair windblown and a smudge darkening one cheek. She circled the car and opened the passenger door.

She bent over and snapped her fingers, reaching for a leash dangling over the edge of the seat.

She tugged. Coaxed.

A nose appeared. Then two front paws, scrabbling backward against the car seat. After more coaxing, followed by another tug, the dog gave up.

It took a high, wide leap straight for her chest, a frothy vision in pink with bows at each ear and an extra big bow at its neck.

Abby staggered, her arms wrapped around the dog's middle. "Easy, Belle. It's okay."

She managed to put the dog down, its leash wrapped tightly around one hand. The animal cowered against her and seemed intent on crawling right back up into her arms.

With gold-and-white spots, freckles and the coat of a golden retriever, it looked like a springer mix. It was the thinnest dog he'd ever seen, though Abby had obviously spent considerable time bathing and brushing it, and the scent of flowery shampoo wafted clear over to the porch.

Abby blew a stray curl out of her eyes. "This is Belle."

He eyed the bows, which would have been over the top even on a poodle. "Fancy."

"The groomer got a bit carried away trying to boost her self-esteem." Abby studied the dog with an expression of devotion. "Belle's a little shy."

Embarrassed over the explosion of pink she wore and longing to roll in roadkill to mute the perfume was probably more like it, but Ethan just smiled. "I put Rufus in the tool-shed with her pups so your dog could settle in. Bring her up in the yard and close the gate so she can explore."

The dog wound around Abby's legs as she headed for the gate. Once inside the yard, she unsnapped the leash and bent to give the dog a reassuring hug. "Go play, Belle," she murmured. "Check the place out."

Belle quivered, one foreleg raised. A moment later she took off around the corner of the house with her tail between her legs.

Abby bit her lip as she watched for her to

return, twisting the leash around her hand. "You're *sure* she can't get out?"

"Absolutely." Ethan stepped off the porch and crossed the lawn to the gate. "Need any help with your things?"

"Not with that arm of yours." She reached out to take his right hand and lifted it to look at the bandage. "Looks like you're keeping it cleaner, now," she said with a note of approval. "I hope you aren't trying to do too much, yet."

"No, ma'am."

"Good. Now, tell me where I should go."

The farther away, the better. The more he'd thought about it, the more awkward this deal seemed. She wasn't an employee, wasn't a guest. Having a woman out here night and day—especially this one—would disrupt the balance he'd established in his life after Barbara left.

Yet, as Keifer had pointed out with a ten-year-old's logic, this was a fair trade. Lodging in exchange for help. And in eight weeks, Keifer would leave with his mom for Minneapolis, so he could get ready for school. Abby would head to some other sort of living situation in town. And life would settle back into the same old comfortable routine.

She cleared her throat. "So, where do you want me?"

"One of the cabins is available until the second week in July. Or, there's a guest room off the kitchen. Less privacy but more convenient, and you wouldn't need to move to the house later."

He'd thought she'd opt for the relative security of the house, but she didn't hesitate. "A cabin, definitely. I'd rather not be underfoot, and I'm sure you'd be more comfortable with that, as well. Right?"

"Are you sure?"

"Are the cabins secure?"

"Dead-bolt locks, and each has a phone. But—"

"How far from the house?"

He nodded toward a stand of trees behind the toolshed. "Maybe fifty yards beyond the shed."

"Perfect."

"You saw the damaged padlocks down by the barn," he said carefully. "So you know that there's been a little trouble up here."

"I'm not a timid woman, Matthews."

"*That* description never crossed my mind."

"So," she said briskly, "let's lay out some ground rules."

"Ground rules?"

"What you expect of me." She had to be Scandinavian, with her pale blond hair and that delicate ivory coloring. A faint pink blush brightened her cheeks. "I'll have to leave by around seven in the morning to get to the hospital. Barring evening meetings, I should be back by six. If my time doesn't cover the full value of that cabin, I'll gladly pay the appropriate amount of rent."

Her blush deepened, and he realized that for all of her attitude, she was actually *flustered.* And—he hated to admit it—she was actually sort of cute when she lost some of her professional veneer.

"I had hired a college student, but she backed out. She was going to keep Keifer company…especially on evenings when I have to be gone. She was also going to help with the cooking and errands. Dusting. Nothing major."

"That works, within the limitations of my hours at the hospital. If you write up a menu, I can certainly make supper."

"Menu?"

"So I know what you want me to use from your pantry and freezer. Now, about my dog. I don't think Belle should roam free because she won't realize this is her home."

As if on cue, Belle slunk around the corner of the house and came over to Abby's side. At the sound of Rufus's excited barking from the toolshed at the far edge of the yard, the dog whined and leaned against Abby's leg.

"She can stay in the fenced yard when you're gone. Otherwise, you could keep her in your cabin during the day."

"Good." Nodding decisively, Abby scanned the surrounding forest. "Now, just tell me where this cabin is, and we'll be set."

Ethan took a long, slow breath and reminded himself why this was such a good deal. It had *seemed* workable enough, until the marines actually landed. Now, the prospect of having Abby here just felt…exhausting.

She eyed him with concern. "Are you feeling all right? Have you had any more chills? Fever?"

"I'm fine."

A small line formed between her brows as

she tapped a finger to her lips. "You know, I'll bet we could set up your IVs and bandage changes right here. You should have—" she paused "—nine more doses of your IV medication. I'm an R.N., so we could get a doctor's order and rent the equipment. That would save you all those trips into town. I could bring everything out tomorrow after work."

A chance to avoid those daily, forty-five-minute trips to town was the best news he'd heard in three days.

Maybe this little arrangement wouldn't be so bad, after all.

ABBY LEANED AGAINST the door of the cabin and closed her eyes as a wave of embarrassment flooded through her. "Good one, Cahill," she muttered under her breath. "Just go ahead. Babble incessantly. Drive the man crazy—and *then* just see if you can find another place to live in this stupid town."

The leering motel guy had made her skin crawl, but coming out here had probably been a bigger mistake. Before, she'd considered Ethan a stubborn, difficult patient. But now, on his own turf, he made her feel...edgy.

There was something almost intimidating about him that couldn't have anything to do with his height or that sharply sculpted, strong-jawed face and day-old stubble shadowing his jaw, it didn't take much imagination to see him dressed for a *GQ* advertisement, with a tux jacket hooked on a finger and slung over his shoulder.

Though of course he hadn't looked at *her* that way. Which was definitely a great relief.

She'd always been take-charge and decisive. Growing up with an absent father and a flighty mother had taught her those skills early on, and they'd served her well.

But tension brought out some of her more irritating flaws—ones her ex-fiancé had been only too happy to point out. Again and again and again. She tended to take over, and then she talked entirely too much.

Jared's voice still echoed through her brain. *Yeah, right. Haul out all those ten-dollar words and see if I'm impressed. I want a wife, not a cold professor.*

As if she sensed Abby's distress, Belle whined and bumped her nose under Abby's hand.

She stroked the dog's silky head. "We're

quite a pair, aren't we? Two homeless gals who just don't fit in."

At a tentative knock on the door she jerked upright and took in a sharp breath.

"Abby? Are you in there?"

Relieved to hear Keifer's voice, she pulled the door open and found him standing outside with a paper grocery sack in his arms.

"Dad said I should bring this, 'cause you're prob'ly busy unpacking and don't have groceries yet. He said we won't see you at breakfast since you have to leave early."

Surprised at Ethan's thoughtfulness, she accepted the offering and looked inside to find a quart of milk, a can of frozen orange juice, bread, a jar of peanut butter and a tub of margarine. "Thanks so much, Keifer. Would you like to come in?"

He edged inside and pulled the screen door shut behind him. "We cleaned this cabin in case you wanted to live here instead of the house. I swept the floor and Dad brought the sheets and stuff. We found *lots* of spiders," he added with obvious relish, "but I caught 'em in a jar and turned 'em loose outside."

"You did a great job. I haven't seen any little visitors so far." She put the groceries away, then folded the paper bag and set it on the counter. "This place is awesome, don't you think?"

The pine-paneled main room was divided into a small kitchen and living area by an L-shaped counter. Two cranberry overstuffed chairs and a sofa faced windows looking out on the pines, and colorful braided rugs added a cozy touch to the hardwood floor. The old TV in the corner struggled to pull in a single, fuzzy station, but there was a VCR and a stack of old movies on the shelf behind.

It was definitely a man's sort of place, with a Pennzoil calendar on the kitchen wall and a giant, framed picture of some sort of terrifying fish over the sofa, but it would be comfortable lodging.

And saying farewell to Hubert this evening, when she'd picked up her things before heading out of town, had filled her with an immeasurable sense of relief.

Keifer wandered over to the small, ivory-painted table and two chairs, where she'd put some delicate blue harebells, deep pink shooting stars and a sprig of fern in an old jelly jar she'd found in the cupboard. "My mom buys flowers at a store. I like these better."

"I found them close by. Wildflowers are my favorite."

He crouched by Belle and crooned to her, stroking her until she thumped her tail against the floor. "She sure doesn't have very nice fur."

"The vet says she's malnourished. She figures someone dumped Belle in the country, so she's been foraging to stay alive."

"That's mean."

"Some people are ignorant. They dump animals thinking that they'll 'have a chance on their own,' but most just get hit by cars or die. Or some farmer has to shoot them because they try to go after farm animals. An animal shelter is a much better place."

"Except they die there, too."

"But at least the staff tries hard to find them homes, and in the meantime, the animals have food and shelter. Some aren't easy to place."

Just this afternoon she'd written out a substantial check to the local shelter and dropped it in the mail. On her way out of town she'd seen Rae on a sidewalk by the drugstore. The girl had hesitated to reveal the name of the vet who'd saved Belle's life, so Abby gave her a quick thank-you note to pass along to him.

Keifer stopped petting the dog and leaned closer to see the raw spot behind her left ear. "Gross!"

"The salve makes it look worse than it is. She has a couple patches like that, but she's on good dog food now. She'll heal pretty fast."

Keifer stood. "We ate already, but Dad said you could come up to the house if you didn't. He could put another hamburger on the grill."

Abby's stomach growled in response. "You know what? That does sound wonderful, but I need to finish unpacking and then I might go to bed early."

"You aren't missing much." Keifer wrinkled his nose. "Whenever I'm here, we have lots of hamburgers and hot dogs."

"Really?" Abby hid a smile. This was certainly good news. Her culinary skills were just a *tad* rusty, so anything beyond Ethan's usual fare might be okay. "Tell your dad thanks for the groceries and offer of supper, okay?"

"Yeah." He hesitated at the door, then grinned at her. "Dad didn't think you'd move out here. He says you're a 'city girl,' so you won't last. Especially 'cause you're out in a cabin by yourself. So we made a bet."

"A *bet?*"

"He said you'd be gone in a week, and I said not. So we each bet five dollars."

Abby laughed. "Really."

"And I think he must be afraid of losing, 'cause he's been pacing all over the house, and he's really grumpy."

Interesting. He'd *encouraged* her to come here. And now he was having second thoughts? "Well, Keifer, I promise you're going to win that bet, because I'm staying until the week after you leave with your mom, just as I promised. Deal?"

He gave her a thumbs-up. "Deal."

She watched him run up the path toward the house, then poured herself a glass of milk and made a peanut butter sandwich.

By tomorrow she'd have her bearings. She'd be able to function like a calm, collected adult, and she'd be in complete control. This would be just fine until the end of summer.

Wolves lurking in the darkness…the isolation…and Ethan Matthews were a small price to pay for a temporary home.

CHAPTER TEN

SHE'D DREAMED of wolves last night. Dark, menacing wolves just outside the cabin. Staring in the windows with eyes that glowed like the embers of a campfire, pulsing and hot.

At midnight she'd awakened to the silence of the woods and felt the eerie stillness settle around her like a cold, damp mantle, the images of the wolves still too vivid. The next time she woke up, Belle was curled at her feet, her warmth comforting.

"Nice, nice puppy," she'd murmured, thankful for the companionship and the trust she'd gained in so short a time.

Now at her desk at the hospital and faced with a pile of documents and a pitiful number of job applications to review, she stifled a yawn and glanced at her watch, willing the hands to move faster.

"Long night?" Erin stood grinning at Abby's door, one hand propped on the frame and a stack of folders in the other arm. "You look beat."

"Bad dreams."

"Ahhh." Erin winked at her. "I hear you moved to the Matthews place."

"I took one of the *cabins,* in exchange for helping out." Abby rubbed her temples. "Do you know how dead-quiet it is, way out there? Other than the occasional hoot of an owl, it's like a tomb."

"I'm out in the country, too, and I love it. But with three kids, it's never quiet during the day." She rested a hand on her belly. "And with baby aerobics going on all night, I can't even imagine getting enough sleep."

"Then come October, you'll be up with feedings. Sounds like fun."

"Your turn will come," Erin retorted, barely suppressing a smile. "But I promise you'll love every minute."

"Nope, I'm a career girl. And that's it." She frowned at Erin's armful of files. "Looks like you're busy."

"I need to review bids for our hospital expansion projects, so I'll be ready for the next board meeting. I can work on this during the drive to Chicago."

"Chicago?"

"Dr. Edwards got us a referral to a surgeon who specializes in congenital leg deformities, in particular, Lily's Talipes Equino Varus." Erin beamed. "We're taking Lily tomorrow."

"That's wonderful news. How's she taking it?"

"It's scary, of course, but she can't wait to walk and run like other kids. She wants her surgery this summer, though I imagine his schedule is full for months. Just getting in so quickly for an evaluation was a true stroke of luck."

The sweet little girl had been born with a clubfoot, and had been in a series of foster homes for years before Erin adopted her. Sadly, the county had failed to provide gradual corrective therapy for her as a young child. "Do you want me to watch the boys while you're gone?"

Erin grinned as she reached across Abby's desk to pat her hand. "That offer is above price, but you're off the hook this time. Grace and Warren are back from their honeymoon tomorrow, and they've offered to stay at our place for a few days." Abby tried not to look too relieved, but Erin laughed. "I know, it will probably be the end of both of them. They'll run away to Florida and never come back."

"Your kids are great, honestly. I just don't have the experience to keep them entertained."

"Just promise you won't ever take them to the animal shelter again." Erin rolled her eyes. "We're now the proud owners of two new cats and a basset, because each child fell in love with something different out there. Connor says *no more.*"

"Oh, my. That means...three dogs, now?"

"It's a big house, but he thinks four kids and five pets are enough." Erin adjusted the load in her arms. "By the way, I got a drug screen report this morning. Our new third-shift nursing applicant flunked."

Which meant her hiring process had come to an abrupt halt. There'd be short staffing until they could hire someone else and ongoing complaints from the existing nurses.

In addition to her administrative duties, Abby would need to help cover shifts on the floor. "That's a shame. Until this, she seemed like such a great find."

Erin nodded. "But one we won't ever be able to consider again."

"I'll get to the other applications first thing."
The phone rang.

"Since Friday's the Fourth of July, I won't
be back in the office until Monday," Erin said
on her way out. "Good luck. Oh, and you can
reach me on my cell if anything comes up."

Abby picked up on the fourth ring. Her
shoulders sagged as Marcia, a first shift
nurse, chattered about an accident Carl had
while painting his house.

He'd suffered a severely sprained ankle…
which meant someone would have to cover
his shifts for perhaps a week.

Abby glanced at the current schedule as
Marcia talked, then reached for the job ap-
plicant files the moment the call ended.
With luck, there'd be someone in this group.
Someone who already lived nearby, who had
a clean record and wanted to start soon.

Because right now, unless other nurses
were able to cover for Carl, Abby would need
to take his three-to-eleven shifts. And that
was going to make for very, very long days.

ABBY STOPPED outside her cabin at midnight,
yawned and rested her head briefly on the
steering wheel.

It had been a long day.

She'd done her own work until three, then she'd donned a uniform and worked Carl's nursing shift until eleven, because no one else was available. Fortunately she'd found a promising job applicant who'd be coming for an interview tomorrow.

But it had also been a very long night, with a heart attack patient who'd been airlifted to Green Bay. A seven-year-old suffering a severe asthma attack. A car accident on the highway that brought in three inebriated teenagers with injuries ranging from broken bones to concussions.

When the boys' parents arrived, the E.R. had turned into a circus, with two parents fighting with each other and assigning blame, while another mom had screamed at her son for ten minutes—until she finally dropped into a chair, awash in tears.

If Connor or Jill had been on call, things would have gone smoother. But tonight had been Dr. Olson's turn and the gruff, elderly physician possessed little tact or sympathy for risk-taking teens. He riled everyone up even more.

Abby cut the lights and turned off her ignition, then stepped out into the damp night air wishing she'd brought a flashlight.

At a rustling sound she whirled around with her hand at her throat, half expecting some sort of wild animal ready to pounce.

"It's only me. Sorry if I scared you," Ethan said. He stood in a pool of moonlight that turned his hair to dark, gleaming pewter and shadowed the hollows of his face.

"Y-you didn't scare me. Not at all."

"Right." His teeth flashed white in the darkness. "I thought you'd like your dog back. She spent the day with Rufus in the yard, and then I brought her inside after dark because she started to whine."

Abby looked down and discovered Belle sitting quietly at his side. "I think she's afraid of the dark." She laughed as she accepted the end of the leash. "I found her on my bed last night."

He cleared his throat. "I'll just wait and make sure you get inside. Keifer was worried about you. He kept checking to see if you were back, but I finally made him go to bed at ten."

"I should have called, but it turned into a hectic night. I'm afraid I won't be much help to you for a while, because I've got to work days and then cover second shift."

"No problem. Though it sure doesn't seem right, you having to do two jobs."

"Yes, well…when Grace—the old director of nursing—retired, three of the old-guard nurses decided to retire right afterward. Coupled with a few other changes and some nurses out with injuries, we've been running short until I can find some new staff. If you can come up with a couple good nurses for me, it's worth a million bucks."

His low laugh seemed to resonate right through her, making their casual conversation seem far too intimate. She took a step back.

"For that kind of compensation, tell me exactly what you want and I'll start looking."

"It's *worth* a million bucks. The actual reward might be somewhat less. Say, a double skinny latte at that coffee shop on Main."

"My favorite place," he said dryly. "Must be all that pink stuff in the windows."

"Or maybe a malt at the drugstore? They have an old-fashioned soda fountain there."

"Nah. Give me fancy coffee and froufrou any day."

She couldn't help but laugh as she tried to envision him in that coffee shop, his broad shoulders dwarfing the delicate, chintz-covered chairs.

"Did Dr. Edwards call you this morning?"

"Yeah. She said to come in today for my IV, so she could examine and rebandage the incision. I understand we can start my treatments at home tomorrow afternoon?"

"Right. And then you'll have just eight days left."

In the soft midnight air, with wisps of fog starting to form at their feet, she was surprised to find out just how comfortable it could be, talking to him.

Maybe too comfortable, because her thoughts were beginning to stray into more personal areas.

He was silent for a long moment, and she had the oddest feeling that he was assessing her—truly looking at her—for the first time. "Go on, get inside," he finally said.

"Thanks, Ethan. For this place. For the groceries, and for taking care of my dog. I definitely owe you."

Inside the cabin she locked the door and

leaned against it, wondering if the past few minutes had just been her imagination.

But Ethan didn't *really* want her here. She was only here to help with some meals and to stay with Keifer when Ethan started going off on his late-evening research jaunts.

Which was fine. She had a great job waiting for her in California, and she certainly wasn't interested in any casual, short-term flings.

Especially not with Ethan Matthews.

ON WEDNESDAY AFTERNOON Ethan flexed his arm to test the confines of the heavy bandage. The doc had promised to start rewrapping it with a much lighter material by Saturday, a week after the accident, if the incision had healed well enough.

He suspected the current bulk was there more as a deterrent against overuse rather than medical need, but when he'd confronted her on Tuesday she'd only smiled.

She apparently had no idea how frustrating it was to be so limited.

The pain was lessening now, but the sutures were itchy and his skin too warm underneath all the gauze. And there were still *two more days.* She probably got some sort of satisfaction from seeing people suffer, he thought grimly. Between her lectures and Abby's, he hoped to never need medical treatment again for as long as he lived.

And he pitied any man who had to be married to either one of them.

He shuffled through the stack of papers on his desk one-handed, looking for the notes he'd taken on the wolf pack in June. Suddenly the stack shifted and half of it slid to the floor.

Muttering under his breath, he glanced at his open bedroom door, where just the tips of Keifer's sneakers were visible, draped over the end of the couch.

The kid played computer games and video games 24/7. At his age, Ethan would have been *outside* 24/7 if his mom hadn't marched him into the house at dusk for supper. Yet Keifer seemed perfectly content to stay inside, with the incomparable northern Wisconsin summer waiting just beyond the porch.

Where was his spirit of adventure? Apparently, held captive by a lot of violent animated characters on a TV screen.

Tempted to remove his bandaging on his own, Ethan eased the rolled-up sleeve of his navy shirt over it—a tight fit—and launched to his feet. "Come on, Keifer, let's get out of this house."

Keifer paused the game. "I thought you had to work."

"I did. I gave up. So let's go play."

"Doing what?"

"We could go fishing on Lake Lunara. We could take the canoe out to Brannock Creek."

"You can't get your arm wet. Abby said so."

"We could go riding, but I don't think I could tighten the girth with one arm."

Keifer's expression became bored.

"What about a hike? There's a trail that leads to a pretty lake just north of here. We could pack a lunch."

"What about going to a movie?"

"That's indoors, sport."

Keifer looked at him as if he'd just spoken Greek. "So?"

"This is a nice summer afternoon, and we should be outside."

Not for the first time, Ethan regretted the minimal time he had with his son. Having him here for just a few weeks every summer plus alternating Thanksgiving and Christmas holidays was in the boy's best interest,

Barbara insisted, given the distance between parents and the limitations of every school year.

Yet there was so much to teach him. So much Ethan wanted to share…and there was so little time to do it. Last year had been even worse. Barbara had kept Keifer over both holidays, so she could take him on trips to the Bahamas and Mexico.

Maybe Keifer had raved about his travels during his phone calls to Blackberry Hill, but at hearing the boy's voice from so far away, Ethan had never felt so lonely.

Keifer's bored expression turned glum. "So that's what you want to do? Go *walking?*"

Ethan curbed his rising frustration. "It's much more than that. Now go put on a long-sleeved shirt and jeans—there are ticks out in the woods—then help me load some food in a backpack."

Keifer rolled off the couch, zapped the TV off with the remote and trudged to his room with the air of someone heading to the gallows.

By the time he reappeared, Ethan had filled a pack with bottled water, snacks, sunscreen and bug repellent, and had been waiting on the porch for five minutes.

"Can we take the dogs?"

"Rufus has to take care of her pups, Keif. She can't go that far."

"Belle? I bet she'd like to go."

At the sound of her name, the dog looked up at them from her shady spot under a lilac bush near the toolshed.

"She isn't ours, and Abby isn't here to give her permission."

"You could call the hospital. Please? I bet Abby would like it if Belle could go, too."

Ethan felt a muscle ticking at the side of his jaw. "We shouldn't disturb her at work. Now let's go."

Grumbling, Keifer closed the yard gate behind him and followed Ethan through the north pasture to a place where a sparkling stream wound through the trees past a tumble of big boulders.

"Pretty cool, isn't it?" Ethan prompted.

"Yeah. So where's the trail?"

"On the other side of our fence." Ethan helped him through the three strands of barbed wire, then led the way up a rocky trail. "I often see deer, foxes and coyotes out here.

Black bears now and then, too, but they're pretty shy."

"Cool."

"We're also entering the range of the Lake Lunara wolf pack, but don't worry. The wolves will give us a wide berth."

"What about the one Abby saw at your house?"

"That might have been a coyote, son."

"No, I think she really did see one, 'cause she sure sounded scared."

"I'll bet she did." Yet she hadn't hesitated to choose a more distant cabin over a guest room in the house. Interesting. "Cityfolk don't know how timid most wolves are when it comes to people."

"I thought they killed things."

"Deer mostly…a pack of four will take down around seventy-two a year."

"There won't be any left!"

Ethan grinned, thankful to finally see a spark of interest. "In this area, cars kill three times more deer than the wolf packs do. And that's just a drop in the bucket compared to the numbers taken by hunters or a harsh winter. Believe me, deer are incredibly prolific."

Keifer fired questions at Ethan all the way to the rocky bluff overlooking the lake. And there, the boy fell silent.

Ethan knew exactly what he was feeling. Knew the feeling well.

He'd been coming out here for five years now, observing a pack that used a den just a hundred yards up the shoreline.

He'd been here at dawn to watch the fog rising from the pristine surface of the lake. He'd seen the lake at midday, sparkling like a brilliant sapphire in a setting of lush green forest. He'd spent countless nights watching the waves glitter silver beneath the moonlight.

Never once had this spot failed to enthrall him. Here, he could almost hear the activities of a long-ago Chippewa village along the shore. Detect the scent of their campfires. See their children playing at the water's edge.

He'd never taken anyone to this place. And though he knew others surely had to know about it, he'd never seen another soul here.

"Are those beaver?" Keifer whispered, pointing to the south shore.

Ethan nodded.

"They're huge!"

"And take a look at the trees they're cutting down. Unbelievable, isn't it?" Ethan handed him a bottle of water and a granola bar. "This isn't the right time to see a lot of animals, though. Dawn and dusk are when most of them come out."

An eagle soared low overhead, then swept upward to land on its perch on a high branch of a pine, his body blending into the dark foliage, his head bright as a white golf ball in contrast. Chattering chipmunks scurried across the rocks, their tails twitching.

"Wow," Keifer breathed. "This is so much better than those dumb parks back home."

"Everything has its own beauty. It's just… different."

"So this is what you do? You come out here and watch things?"

The simplification of his meticulous research made Ethan smile. "In a manner of speaking."

On the way home, Keifer was silent, watching his surroundings with a far more careful eye. As they drew close to the house, he looked up at Ethan with a troubled expression. "This was way cool, Dad. I wish—" he swallowed "—I wish you wanted me here more often."

Momentarily stunned, Ethan didn't know quite what to say.

"I know you're busy and stuff. It's okay."

Did a guy hug a kid who was ten? Would it be an embarrassment to fledgling masculine pride? Ethan kicked himself for not having a better understanding of what made his own son tick, then dropped the backpack and gave Keifer a bear hug anyway.

Stepping back, he rested his hands on the boy's thin shoulders. "I love having you here. Every last minute. I swear, it's the very best part of my year."

Keifer lifted his gaze from his shoes. "You didn't care about seeing me last year, at Christmas and Thanksgiving."

A pain settled deep into Ethan's chest. "That was because you had a chance for some wonderful trips with your mom. They just happened to be the same year." He'd been gracious, trying to put Keifer's best interests above his own, but it hadn't been easy. "But, hey, it isn't going to happen again. Okay? And we've got all the rest of the summer—more time than we usually have. So let's make the best of it, okay?"

Keifer nodded, his eyes once again averted.

"Want to race to the house?"

Keifer took off in a flash, disappearing around a bend and leaving Ethan laughing as he jogged along behind him.

But a second later, he heard the boy cry out in dismay.

By the time he came in sight of the house, Keifer was running down the lane to the road, calling Belle's name.

They'd carefully closed and latched the gate when they left, but now it was wide open. Rufus was in the shed, with just the tip of her nose showing out the door. Growling.

And Belle was nowhere to be seen.

CHAPTER ELEVEN

KEIFER STARED at the gate and wished he could melt into the ground and disappear.

This day had been one of the best he could remember. A whole afternoon with Dad, talking about good stuff—not just the usual *"Hey, how are you? How's school?"* that made up most of their awkward phone conversations through the year.

But somehow he'd screwed up the latch, Abby's dog was gone and Dad was coming up the lane with a scowl on his face that promised trouble. Keifer felt an ache deep in his chest, knowing he'd just lost something important—the kind of man-to-man ease between them that he'd seen other guys share with their own dads.

"I…thought it was latched, honest. I pulled it shut." He held his breath as Dad stopped at the open gate and inspected the sturdy U-shaped latch that should have held the pipe-framed gate securely, then his words came out in a rush. "I never meant for Abby's dog to get loose. I'll go find her, honest. She can't be very far."

Dad gave him an odd look and rested one big hand on his shoulders. "I heard you close the gate, son. I know you took care of it."

"B-but…"

"She might have bumped the gate just right, and lifted that latch with her nose. It's okay. Belle has been fed here, and there's nothing but forest and open land for miles. She'll probably come back when she gets hungry."

Keifer closed his eyes, remembering how much Abby loved her new dog. "We should still try to find her, shouldn't we? I mean, Abby trusted that she'd be okay. What if Belle just keeps going?"

"We've got plenty of daylight. We could drive down the road both ways, and if she doesn't turn up by tomorrow we could file a report at the animal shelter. I don't think she's likely to get that close to civilization, though. Not from clear out here."

Keifer shuddered, remembering Abby's worry over getting to the shelter in time to save her dog. "I sure hope we find her before then. Can we go now?"

Dad dropped his backpack just inside the gate. "We'll have to start always using this, too," he said, unsnapping a length of chain hanging from the chain-link fence and fastening it around the gate for good measure. He pulled a set of keys from his jeans pocket. "Let's go."

"BELLE'S *gone?*" Her face pale and weary, Abby shut the door of her car. "For how long?"

"Midafternoon. She was in the yard when we went hiking and must have bumped the hook open with her nose. Keifer was still upset when he went to bed. He thinks it's his fault."

Abby had left by seven in the morning. Once again, she'd pulled in at midnight. Silver in the moonlight, her hair had escaped in tendrils from the knot on top of her head, and her eyes looked huge and dark.

She looked so fragile, he had to fight an unexpected urge to put an arm around her and pull her close. Which, of course, would be a very bad idea.

"I'll be gone before he gets up, but tell him I'm not upset with him, okay? Things happen." She managed a reassuring smile. "Belle was a stray, so she probably figured out her escape methods long ago. I just hope she comes back."

"We did spend a couple hours looking. We drove to the end of our road, then back toward town. After supper, Keifer rode Buddy bareback through the pastures calling for her, and I jogged several miles down our closest trails. No luck."

From the horizon, in the direction of Lake Lunara, he could hear wolves howling faintly. Other wolves howled from much farther to the west—barely audible.

Abby seemed to sense his watchfulness, because she turned toward the sound and her shoulders tensed. "Will they go after my dog?" she asked quietly.

"Mostly they hunt deer, and a fair number of beaver in the fall and spring."

"But on occasion…"

"A wolf that ignores the scent and howl messages of another pack's territory trespasses at risk of death. A roaming dog faces the same risk."

"Poor Belle."

"Mostly hunting dogs, though. The wolves probably consider the baying of a hound a territorial challenge."

"But they still might go after her, right?"

"Maybe. There's been farm dog depredation, but it certainly isn't common."

Abby sounded so heartbroken that he let himself rest a hand on her shoulder. Her warmth radiated through her thin cotton scrub top and landed dead-center in his chest, reminding him of all the reasons he'd kept careful distance.

He cleared his throat and eased away to lean one hip against the rear fender of her car. "That doesn't mean Belle won't come back. She could turn up on your step first thing in the morning."

"I sure hope so." She stepped around him and opened the trunk of her car. "Sorry I wasn't here to help with Keifer or supper this evening. I do have the IV equipment and antibiotic for you, though."

She lifted out the base of an IV stand and handed it to him, then gathered up the top section of the stand and a cardboard box.

Well, this certainly looked like fun. "Your place or mine?"

She shrugged. "We're closer to the cabin. It won't take long, since you already have a heplock in place."

"Makes me feel like a bionic man," he said.

She settled him at the kitchen table, hung a bag of saline and with quick, professional efficiency set up the small bag of antibiotic, then unwrapped his IV site and swabbed the rubber port thoroughly with an alcohol pad. In a few moments she had the antibiotic running. He leaned back to watch the steady drip, drip, drip of the fluid.

"I still think they could've given me a bottle of pills."

"Not of the antibiotic the doctor ordered. This is the only way. And believe me, with the kind of soft tissue damage you had, the potential for infection was a big concern." She carefully unwrapped his dressing, inspected the incisions and redressed them. "Looks good. No heat, redness or other signs of infection."

He watched her straighten up her supplies. Her scrub top was covered with cartoon characters in primary colors; the baggy bottoms were electric-blue. Definitely meant to put toddlers at ease, the whimsical motif made her look like an escapee from a three-ring circus…incongruous considering her crisp efficiency.

"The nurses tell me your surgeon has done some amazing facial reconstructions, so apparently he's very talented. You should have very little scarring on your arm," she said as she returned to look at the IV drip. "How are you feeling?"

"Impatient."

She rolled her eyes. "I wouldn't have guessed."

She flicked the IV line to flush the last of the med through, watched in concentration, then disconnected the line and flushed the port to keep the heplock open until his next dose.

"There you go. We might as well leave all of this here, unless you want to take it up to your house."

"Leave it." He stretched, stood.

The cabin was utilitarian at best, but she'd gathered a bouquet of wildflowers for the table and a velvety quilt in mossy green and rose was draped over the sofa. A candle she'd just lit on the kitchen counter scented the air with lily of the valley.

He and Keifer had left it clean, smelling of eau de Pine-Sol. In just forty-eight hours, Abby had made it a—

He smothered a laugh. "Hey, where's the lake trout?"

The framed painting had been hanging over the sofa when he'd bought the place. He'd never gotten around to pitching it; it had to be one of the worst pieces of art in the entire state. The painting had eventually grown on him, though, because every time he studied it, it seemed unbelievably worse.

"The trout?"

"It hung above the sofa. A wonderful ex- ample of regional art." He thought he heard her snort, but when he turned to look at her, her face was perfectly innocent.

"That's what I thought," she murmured. "*Very* regional art."

"In fact, I had a collector up here who gave me a bid on it."

At that, she gave up and laughed. "I'll just bet he did." She tipped her head toward the living area. "It's behind the sofa now. I swear, those googly fish eyes followed me around the room. They were too eerie for words."

"Well, there's no accounting for taste," he said, which made her laugh even harder.

It was late.

Well after midnight.

She needed to be up early in the morning and he needed to leave. Yet he found it hard to simply walk out the door.

She could laugh at herself, and at him.

She could give her time without hesitation, even when she had to be exhausted.

And she could learn that the dog she loved was missing, and not lay blame.

But Abby would be leaving in a few months and he would definitely be staying.

Time to go home.

She tipped her head and looked at him. "What?"

"Nothing—nothing at all."

The moment stretched out, marked by his quickening pulse and temptation to find out if her lips would be as soft as he imagined.

Her gaze drifted down to his mouth, as if she was caught in the same spell.

And then her dimples deepened and she flashed a bright smile. "I think I must be falling asleep on my feet," she said. "And morning comes way, way too early around here."

"Right." He headed for the door, raising his good arm in farewell. Halfway there he stopped, recalling Keifer's demand at bedtime. "We're going to watch the fireworks on Friday. Keif—uh, we wondered if you'd like to join us."

Her eyes widened and her smile slipped a little. "Wow. It's been *years* since I've done that. Thanks."

The invitation clearly touched her, and he realized that she was going to be alone out in her cabin now that her dog was gone, and perhaps she wasn't feeling quite so brave anymore. "That guest room in the house is still open, if you decide you'd like more civilization."

Her chin lifted. "I'm perfectly fine, but I do appreciate the offer."

With a nod, he left and sauntered down the moonlit path to the house, whistling as he made his way through the trees.

And found himself looking forward to the Fourth of July.

ABBY HAD WORRIED about Belle since last evening. She'd hoped that the dog would show up, but this morning there'd been no friendly face at her door, no wagging tail... just the chatter of chipmunks and the scattering of a few squirrels when she'd called Belle's name.

With Erin and Connor gone to Chicago and Dr. Olson leaving this morning for a three-day continuing education meeting at a golf resort near Madison, it was only Dr. Edwards, Dr. Leland Anderson and her for the weekly breakfast meeting at Ollie's.

A meeting Abby hoped would last half the usual time, so she could run home to check for Belle before her day at the hospital started.

Leland, as fastidious as ever, slowly sipped at his coffee and neatly placed the cup back on the saucer, then clasped his slender hands. "There really isn't much point in meeting today, with two doctors and our administrator gone."

"Except that Ollie's cinnamon rolls are incomparable." Jill savored another sticky morsel. "Though coming here is all for the good of the hospital, of course."

"Which brings up a good point," Leland

retorted. "We're working at bringing in specialists from Green Bay. We've been remodeling, and will have that MRI unit installed within two months. But we still aren't getting the staff we need." He looked over his half glasses at Abby, his mouth a thin, disapproving line. "I covered the E.R. last weekend, and the nurses had been run ragged. I heard them complain that nothing is being done. I realize you're just an interim DON, but what's the problem?"

Abby put down her fork and gave him a level look. "We've gotten some applicants, but most back away because of the benefit package and pay scale."

"No interviews this week?"

"Three. Two weren't quite what we're looking for. One…flunked her drug test."

"Just *three?*"

Abby curbed her frustration. "We've got to convince the hospital board to raise salaries and improve the benefits, or we're never going to be competitive."

"The hospital has been struggling, Abby. There are other benefits to living up here— it's a vacation paradise. Maybe you haven't been selling all of the *positives* to these people."

Jill jerked a napkin out of the dispenser. "Believe me, she's not only working on that, but she's also pulling second shift duty after a full day in management. For someone who's here short-term, she's giving a hundred-fifty percent."

He dipped his head in acquiescence. "That may well be. But I've got another issue that's come up…and I'm more than concerned. When we're done here I'd like to talk to you privately, Abby."

"Sure." Mystified, she caught Jill's eye, but Jill just shrugged. "If this is about the hospital, though, I think we should talk about it right now."

He splayed his hands on the table. "I don't think—"

"Please. This is a very private area. Whatever you have to say will stay right here."

"Very well. As a member of the board, I try to be vigilant about potential problems, and right now, if a state inspector was to walk through our front door, we could get dinged on violations any first year nursing student knows to avoid."

"I'm not sure what you mean," Abby said slowly. "Have you found discrepancies with the med passes? Patient care?"

"Charting." He lowered his voice. "I did my rounds early this morning and the initial nursing assessments weren't done on the two patients who came in last night."

Abby's mouth fell open. "Of course they were. That's the first step with every admission, and I was there covering a shift. I filled out those forms myself."

"Maybe things got too hectic, and you set them aside to do later."

"I *clearly* remember doing them, and I put them in the charts. Ask Dr. Olson."

"I'll do that when he gets back to town." Leland's voice grew excessively slow and patient. "I understand this job would be challenging to someone coming from an educational setting. It's just not the same now, is it?"

"Of course not. But I assure you—"

"And another thing…about the corrections in your charting," he tsked-tsked as he shook his head, "you surely know the protocol regarding this."

"Corrections?"

"It's universal medical procedure, in every hospital policy manual I've ever seen. A simple, thin line through the error that doesn't obliterate the original, and an 'M.E.' initialed there for Medical Error. Not," he added firmly, "scribbles that hide the original, and that might be perceived as covering up a serious error. That could open us up to all sorts of trouble if there's ever a medical review."

Uneasy, she thought back over the two shifts she'd covered as an R.N. during the past two days. With the exception of one miswritten word—which she'd dealt with per standard protocol—she couldn't remember any corrections. "I'm well aware of that."

"Good."

But the censorious tone in his voice and the quick second glance he gave Jill said it all. He not only believed she'd been ignorant, but that perhaps she'd been trying to mask some sort of error on her part—and now wasn't owning up to the truth.

She hadn't cared much for the man before. Opinionated, always the devil's advocate and cynical about the improvements at the hospital, he'd made her uncomfortable since their first meeting.

As a member of the board he would've seen her application. Since he seemed to be absorbed by every last, persnickety detail of anything that crossed his radar, he had to remember that she'd had three years of clinical nursing experience before going back to college, and had worked weekends in an E.R. until she'd completed her degrees.

Yet he'd just accused her of ignorance and incompetence, over incidents that hadn't even occurred. "Where did you find these altered progress notes?"

His eyes narrowed. "The Ferguson chart. Interdisciplinary progress notes. But it isn't anything you can fix."

She struggled for an even tone. "Of course not. I just need to see what was done, because I've *never* made the types of errors you've described."

Jill quickly steered the conversation toward the annual Fourth of July parade, the street dance following the fireworks and the holiday sailboat race out on Sapphire Lake. Abby nodded now and then as she considered Leland's accusation.

When the discussion wound down, she cleared her throat. "I just want to add one thing. Leland believes those missing assessments and charting errors are my fault. But my question is—who else could've done it…and why? Maybe it'll happen again, and one of these days, a patient's life could be at stake."

"I agree," Jill said firmly. "I think we'd all better keep our eyes open. Because heaven knows, our hospital has had enough trouble as it is."

CHAPTER TWELVE

THE FOURTH OF JULY. Who knew that this All-Amercan holiday could trigger such strong, mixed feelings?

Six months ago Abby had been planning her wedding for this Fourth of July weekend. Three months later—after every last detail had been planned right down to the flower girl's lace gloves and the artfully designed appetizers to be passed on silver trays—Jared had left a message on her answering machine. A *message,* the coward.

Four days later he was on a plane to Cancun for a whirlwind honeymoon with some woman he'd met at a dental convention, leaving Abby to cancel plans and placate her horrified mother.

Abby's anger at Jared had lasted a week. After that, she'd felt only relieved to escape such a close call with a man she couldn't trust…coupled with anger at herself for being so utterly, undeniably stupid. She'd completely misjudged him, swayed too easily by his good looks and easy charm. He'd become a long and comfortable habit until they'd both taken it for granted that they'd eventually be picking out silver patterns.

But how could she have missed all the signs of trouble along the way?

"A nickel for your thoughts," Ethan said over Keifer's head, from his side of the blanket they'd spread out on the grass.

"Um…the weather. It's definitely a nice night to be out here."

"Good weather?" He grinned wryly. "That would certainly account for the grim expression."

"And, truthfully, I've been worrying about Belle all day. What if she's hurt? Hungry? What if…" She couldn't bring herself to say the words.

"Keifer and I both went looking again today. We hiked for several hours, and also went out in the truck." He frowned. "It's hard to believe she'd take off like that, unless she took out after a rabbit and just went too far to find her way back."

"If she was a stray long enough, maybe she

learned to hunt to stay alive." Though she'd been so gaunt, she sure hadn't been very good at it. "And it's only been a couple days, now. I still have hope."

Keifer leaned forward to grab a Mountain Dew out of the cooler and swatted at a mosquito with his other hand. He watched a couple of boys saunter past.

"Hey," the taller redhead said to him without breaking stride.

"Hey." Keifer's face fell when the two kept walking.

He settled back on his elbows and stared glumly at the sky. "It's almost dark. Aren't the fireworks supposed to start?"

"Another twenty minutes, probably. Do you want a hot dog?" Ethan reached for the back pocket of his faded denims and pulled a five out of his wallet. "Do you want anything, Abby?"

She shook her head. "No thanks."

She'd been up early and at the hospital by eight this morning, hoping to get done in time to get back to Ethan's to finally make a supper. Instead, with a multicar pileup out on the highway and short staffing, she'd ended up working until almost eight. Even now, her senses humming with residual adrenaline, the thought of eating made her stomach tense.

Keifer accepted the money and bounded down the knoll to the park baseball diamond, where a concession stand had drawn long lines since they'd arrived.

Ethan propped an elbow on the blanket and rested his head against his palm to watch him go. "This is the first time he's been here for the Fourth. I imagine he's missing his friends and the much bigger celebration down in Minneapolis."

"Does he know any kids up here?"

"No."

"Maybe you could introduce him to Erin Reynolds's kids. They're close to the same age, I think. He certainly wouldn't have a quiet moment with those three around."

"Aren't those the ones who got you evicted?"

Abby laughed. "Only because my landlord had zero tolerance for noise. He even thought I was rowdy, so you have to factor that into your assumption about Erin's boys. Lily is just a lamb."

A sudden bang reverberated through the air, followed by a blinding flash and an earthshaking explosion Abby felt clear to her bones.

A second later, another rocket launched upward with a loud whoosh—and this time, a sparkling sphere of red stars filled the sky overhead. A collective gasp of delight rose from the crowd.

"Beautiful," Abby breathed. "I haven't seen fireworks in years."

Ethan nodded, watching the crowd near the concession stand. "Looks like Keifer found some kids to hang out with."

Sure enough, he was standing with the boys who'd passed by earlier. All three stared up at the sky with rapt attention. "That should make this even better for him. Oh, look!"

A thick shower of diamonds shot high into the air, splitting into multiple branches that arced far out over the park. The next shell produced crackling sparks and intense bursts of light followed by an explosion that rained silver ribbons of stars.

Ethan eased onto his back and, mindful of his bandaged arm, stacked his hands beneath his head to watch the show. "How come you didn't spend the holiday with relatives?"

"Detroit was a tad far, and I certainly don't have any vacation time."

"Still, it's a three-day weekend. Do you have a lot of family back there?"

"Parents. A few cousins. The rest of the family is out east."

Though Detroit wasn't quite far enough away. Her parents' disapproval over her summer plans and her future job in California was still too fresh. And just in case she might forget, in their weekly phone calls they still begged her to rethink her decision, come home and be *sensible*.

There were even murmurs about coming up to see her.

Abby sighed. At thirty-two, she was still subject to parental lectures on life, and it was getting just a little old. "So how about you?" she asked, fending off any more questions with a parry of her own. "Local?"

"Grew up in Minnesota. Worked there, Wyoming and Montana before moving here."

Curious, she turned to look at him. "I'm not even sure what you are…or do."

He shifted uncomfortably, then gave up and stood, hooking a thumb in his back pocket. He scanned the crowd during each burst of light until he picked out his son. His shoulders relaxed. "Wildlife biologist, mostly. I've dabbled in a few other things along the way. I'm on a sabbatical right now, of sorts."

Keifer had mentioned something about Ethan taking photographs for a book, so she waited, wondering if he would say anything. But he just stared up at the sky. "Peony," he said. "Nice one."

She got to her feet, too. "What?"

"That last shell. The stars fly outward and then drift down. No tails. The Willow droops, too, but the falling stars have thick, sparkling trails."

He was far more informative about the fireworks than himself. Typical man.

Which, she reminded herself, had been one of the bigger problems with Jared. No information. And where did it get her? Canceled florists and photographers and testy three-piece string ensembles, and a dizzying amount of lost deposits.

The darkness, interspersed with flashes of light, created a sense of intimacy despite the crowd farther down the slope. Even in the poor lighting she was all too aware of just how close Ethan was.

She suddenly wished Keifer was back on the blanket between them.

Another dozen brilliant explosions of color filled the sky before she noticed Ethan watching her instead of the show. "What?"

"I was just wondering why a woman like you isn't married with six kids."

"You mean, a woman my age," she said dryly.

"At whatever age."

"For one thing, I'm not the maternal type. For another…" She hesitated a moment too long over the half truth. "I've always thought my career was more important than picking up someone's socks."

"Ever been married?"

"No!"

"Engaged, then." His dimples deepened. "Definitely engaged."

"I…was. Big mistake. Very big."

"Ah."

"It all comes down to having the right priorities. Making careful decisions based on thoughtful and thorough analysis. I think—"

A moment ago he'd been an arm's length

away. Now he seemed to loom over her. He gently cupped her chin in his hand. "Thinking is a good thing," he murmured, his eyes locked on hers. "But sometimes, impulse is even better."

His hand was calloused, warm. His hazel eyes glittered with the reflection of the light bursting overhead. The laugh lines at the corners of his eyes deepened as he flashed a faint grin and then lowered his mouth to hers for a brief kiss.

Her breath caught. She blinked, and it took a moment before she could gather her scattered thoughts. "I—I don't think that was a good idea."

Another lie, because nothing had *ever* felt so good. So absolutely right. Even now, there was a distinct possibility he'd just shorted out her entire autonomic nervous system, because her heart still wasn't hitting on all four cylinders.

He took a step back, his face a mask of regret. "Sorry. I probably shouldn't have done that."

She'd always been practical. Unemotional. She considered the analysis of cost versus benefit a logical approach to most things in life, and with the exception of her blindness where Jared had been concerned, she usually made wise and defensible decisions. But there was something about Ethan kissing her that made her want to throw caution to the winds.

"Again," she demanded. She pulled him closer, her hands framing his lean face.

Finally, he pulled away with a sound of regret.

"I...just wanted to make sure," she managed to say. "I thought maybe it was my imagination." She took a steadying breath. "But of course, you're absolutely right. This was a mistake, and we certainly shouldn't repeat it."

She leaned down to gather her purse, thankful for the darkness and hoping it hid the warmth in her cheeks. "I...think I'll check on Keifer."

Another fireworks shell shot into the air as she hurried down the hill. Three or four deafening reports shook the ground, then it burst into colorful sparkling streamers.

When the reverberation faded she thought she heard Ethan chuckle. Well, so be it. He probably thought she was running from him, but nothing could be further from the truth.

She was running from herself.

"CAN'T WE GO LISTEN to the band? Just for a while? *Please?*"

Keifer jogged backward in front of Ethan with a sticky cone of cotton candy in one hand. "Troy told me they blocked off a whole section of Main Street!"

"Careful, you're going to fall." Sure enough, Keifer's shoe caught on something and he started to pitch over. Ethan caught and steadied him. "It's already after ten, son."

"Like that's bedtime or something? It's Friday night and I'm *ten years old.*"

The kid had arrived from Minneapolis with a cocky attitude that gradually faded. After an hour with those other boys at the fireworks, some of that attitude was back. "We've still got a long drive home, and I haven't done evening chores yet."

The park was on the edge of town, a good six blocks from Main, but even here the music was loud. Downtown, it had to be deafening. Ethan hesitated when they reached his truck. How often did the boy get to enjoy a live band? Would he ever be here for another Fourth of July?

"Abby, do you mind? I know you had a long day at work. Maybe just a half hour?"

She'd avoided meeting his eyes since that error of judgment during the fireworks. No wonder. He'd probably startled her, kissing her like that. And what right did he have, anyway? She was simply a boarder at his place. Living out at his isolated place, she was probably more afraid of him than she'd ever been of the wildlife.

And then she'd kissed him back... Why she'd done that, he didn't know, but he'd had a hard time pulling away. *But it's a good thing I did it anyway. Life is too complex as it is,* he told himself.

She rounded the front of the truck for the passenger side, scooted Keifer in first and climbed in after him. "If you want to go listen to the band, it's fine with me."

Ethan eased into the slow train of bumper-to-bumper vehicles exiting the park and took a back street into town. Sure enough, he found a parking space in the First Methodist parking lot a block from the dance, despite the tourists jamming the streets.

"Now stay close," he warned Keifer as they reached the barricaded section of Main. Hundreds of people were already out on the street, dancing to a fair rendition of an Elvis oldie. "I know you're a big guy, but I don't want to search for hours to find you. Okay?"

Keifer nodded, his eyes already scanning the crowd for his newfound friend. Sure enough, a red-haired boy grinned at him and beckoned. "I'll just be over there. Promise!"

Before Ethan could reply, Keifer wound his way through the tightly packed crowd.

"I shouldn't have given in," Ethan muttered under his breath as waves of more people arrived.

"I'll help keep tabs on him," Abby shouted over the noise as she moved forward. "But look, it seems like a pretty sedate crowd. He'll be fine."

Fine maybe, but not that easy to find. He watched her disappear into the crowd, calling Keifer's name.

There were plenty of gray-haired folks out on the street, merrily fox-trotting to rock. Young kids were flinging each other around and acting silly while lovestruck teens danced way too slow and far too close despite the fast beat.

And somewhere, Keifer was lost in this mass of people.

The hair at the back of Ethan's neck stood up. He turned slowly, bumping into a bulky, violet-haired woman and her Ichabod Crane companion.

A trio of tall, burly young men lounged against the corner of the drugstore, their bare arms thick with dark tattoos. Late teens or early twenties, probably, exuding arrogant belligerence.

If he remembered right, they'd been among the four poachers he'd caught on government land last winter.

One of them glared back at him, poked his buddy in the ribs and then the second one stared, too.

It wouldn't be any surprise if they'd been the ones to tamper with his padlocks...or if they'd had something to do with the dead calf.

But he'd called the sheriff's office about the padlocks, and there'd been no fingerprints and no proof.

Besides, there were other possible suspects in the area. A couple of farmers who'd turned in highly suspect wolf-depredation claims that he'd denied back when he'd still been working for the state, and who'd resented his stand on the wolves ever since. There were also some guys in town who'd claimed their hunting dogs had been killed by wolves, but again, no proof.

Gritting his teeth, Ethan scanned the crowd for Keifer, then started toward the drugstore.

But before he'd made it halfway through the shoulder-to-shoulder crowd, the three guys had disappeared.

ABBY GLANCED OVER her shoulder to where Ethan had been, but saw only a press of people moving toward the dance area. Grace had mentioned the huge influx of tourists every summer. Every one of them and their brother had to be here right now.

Nervous, she craned her neck to look for the top of Keifer's strawberry-blond head. Nothing—but he was a good head or two shorter than the adults here. She pushed on in the direction where she'd seen him last. The kid with the red hair was taller, fortunately, and she'd caught sight of him just a moment ago.

With luck, she could collar Keifer and haul him back to his dad, and then they could all escape to the blessed silence and peace of the country.

Where she could flee to her cabin, lock the door and wallow in her utter embarrassment over what she'd done. After a month or two, she might actually be able to face Ethan again without blushing ten shades of red.

She stumbled over someone's foot, caught a passing sleeve to right herself. Apologizing profusely, she edged forward until she reached the corner of Main and Elm. Ahead, the crowd thinned and the streets were dark. But hadn't the redhead gone this direction?

She stopped to scan the sidewalks.

Someone lurched into her, nearly knocking her off her feet. She staggered into the trunk of a tree, its rough bark clawing at her shoulder.

An unfamiliar man loomed close, and she was assailed by a miasma of stale beer, sweat and tobacco as he exhaled a bleary, "'Scuse me," inches from her face.

But despite the alcoholic stench of him, his small, narrowed eyes were alert and a smirk twisted his thick lips. "Bad company you're keeping, if you ask me. Better be careful, Sugar." He stared at her, then moved on, his gait unsteady.

She watched him until he disappeared into the crowd, her pulse hammering and her hands trembling. He'd been drinking, but that hadn't been the half-conscious rambling of some drunk.

She'd heard the threat in his voice and she'd seen it in his eyes, and now Blackberry Hill no longer seemed like a safe place to be.

Spotting Keifer and his friend at last, she hurried across the street. "Your dad and I have been looking for you, Keifer. It's time to go home."

CHAPTER THIRTEEN

THE DAY AFTER the Fourth of July, Abby had stopped by the outpatient clinic as Dr. Edwards removed Ethan's heavy bandaging, to announce that one of the nurses was coming back to work sooner than expected after medical leave, so she could start getting home in time to make supper and stay with his son.

For the past eleven days she'd been doing just that.

They'd lost their easy banter though, a casualty of the kiss Ethan couldn't quite bring himself to regret.

Because, beneath her proper, cool and authoritative shell, was a woman who could knock his socks off with just a kiss.

Given that she barely acknowledged his presence now, though, it wasn't likely he'd ever experience it again.

Even when she was delivering his daily IV meds—which had ended last Wednesday—

she'd been calmly professional. Distant. And he'd tried to be the same.

But that distance was going to change.

"Did you tell her about Ralph?" Ethan asked as he rinsed the last supper plate and stowed it in the dishwasher.

"Nope." Keifer finished wiping the kitchen table and looked across the room to where Abby was pummeling a football-size lump of bread dough.

She'd been dutifully making supper almost every night, though she hadn't been kidding when she said she wasn't a great cook. And then she stayed until Ethan returned—usually around midnight—before heading to her own cabin.

But she'd been tense and jittery, and she certainly wasn't one to chatter.

And given the way she was working that dough, this was probably going to be another loaf of bread with the digestibility of an anvil.

Ethan gave Keifer an encouraging smile. "Go ahead. Tell her."

"You, Dad. Your job."

Abby dropped the dough into a big bowl and draped a towel over it, then turned toward them with her hands on her hips. "What?"

"Remember when we talked about our deal?"

"Right."

"Tomorrow's the day."

"What day—?" Her gaze flew to the over-size calendar on the wall, and her shoulders slumped. "The cabin. I've been so busy, I just forgot."

"Both cabins will be full starting tomorrow afternoon, Abby, but you're still welcome to the guest room here in the house. Or, if you're not comfortable with that, we can consider our deal done."

"I promised I'd stay through the summer." She sighed heavily. "But would you rather I left? I could try to find a place in town. With-out Belle, maybe I—"

"Stay, Abby."

"Yeah, stay," Keifer chimed in. "We'll be stuck with hamburgers and hot dogs if you go…and what would I do when Dad's gone at night?"

She stood silent for a long moment, appar-ently weighing her options. "Then I guess I'd better move my things to the house tonight, because I'll be at work all day tomorrow."

"I'll help, and Dad can, too."

She laughed, but there was little humor in her eyes. "No problem, pal. Now that I have my car back from the shop, I've got plenty of room. I can toss everything in the trunk."

"I'll help anyway," Keifer insisted.

Ethan looked down and realized that he'd been white-knuckling the back of a kitchen chair, sure that Abby would decide to go back to town.

It was hard to imagine coming into the house at six and not finding something simmering away on the stove. Or coming home late at night and not finding her with her nose in a book, curled up at the end of the sofa.

But it would only last until the end of August, he said to himself as he followed Abby and Keifer out the door. What would it be like when both of them were gone?

He didn't want to imagine.

ABBY UNPACKED THE LAST of her clothes and stowed them away in a drawer, then shook out her favorite comforter onto the bed. The guest room was pleasant really, with its antique mahogany four-poster and matching mirror-topped bureau, and it had its own half-bath for privacy. Its location just off the kitchen was perfect, because Ethan and Keifer were both in a distant part of the house.

She was grateful for a decent place to stay, even if it was a long drive into work every morning, and the free room and board meant she could save even more toward the high cost of real estate in California.

The difficulty was staying in the same house as Ethan. He'd certainly been offhand about that embarrassing moment in the park a couple weeks ago. It hadn't meant a thing to him, but she'd made an absolute fool of herself—with hundreds of people nearby.

And apparently some of them had noticed.

Since then, she'd received some good-natured ribbing at the hospital about that kiss, and even a few raised eyebrows among the older staff.

But they could all think what they liked. Moving to Ethan's cabin had helped her save Belle, and moving into the main house would give her a greater sense of security now that her dog was gone.

Hearing a knock, she turned to find Ethan standing at her door, backlit by the single light she'd left on over the kitchen sink. "Have everything you need?"

"Thanks for the queen-size sheets. Mine are in storage back in Detroit."

"Help yourself to anything you need from the linen closet."

"Thanks."

An awkward silence lengthened between them until he finally flashed a grin. "We're glad you decided to stay."

"This works well for me, too. An even trade."

"And…" He seemed to choose his next words with care. "I want you to know you're perfectly safe here. Things got a little out of hand at the fireworks, but it won't happen again."

"Certainly not." She smiled to soften her words. "It was just one of those crazy things. It was dark and the fireworks were romantic. That's all."

"Good. Friends?"

She accepted his handshake and ignored the warm tingles that raced up her arm. "Absolutely. Nothing more than that."

WITH SUMMER in full swing, Ethan's two cabins were filled by a constant rotation of fishermen. They came alone or with their buddies, prepared their own meals and fished from dawn until past dusk. For those who contracted his services, Ethan served as a fishing guide.

While working as a wildlife biologist he'd restricted these fishing expeditions to evenings and weekends. This summer, he'd scheduled them more often. And now that he was free of his bandages and his arm was nearly healed, he was finally able to follow through.

The wealthy clients who came from Minneapolis or Chicago with five-hundred-dollar fly rods from Cabelas were willing to pay exorbitant rates for guaranteed success.

He knew every lake, every stream in the region like the layout of his own house. And with myriad live insects darting over the water, one needed an especially enticing fly and the right presentation technique.

So he helped his clients hone their casting skills and took them to the right spots at the right time of day, gauging the water temperature and selecting the best flies for that moment.

Ralph, a retired neurosurgeon with a keen

eye but slowly advancing Parkinson's, was one of his favorite clients.

"I see you've got your boy with you now," Ralph said as he lifted a last duffel bag and his fly rod case out of his trunk. "Cute kid."

"Thanks." Ethan bent to pick up a duffel and tackle box.

"Whoa—maybe I'd better get that." Ralph settled his glasses higher on his nose and inspected the angry, dark pink lattice of surgical scars on Ethan's arm. "What did you do, play with a shark?"

"Auger." Ethan headed for the cabin and held the door for Ralph.

Ralph looked closer at the wounds and nodded in approval. "Someone did a good job of sewing you back up. In time, those scars will barely show."

"I just wanted it to heal fast."

"So are we still on for tomorrow?"

"You bet. With a slight problem, though. I can take you out at dawn, but my son would have to come along because he can't stay home alone. Otherwise, we could go in the evening, when there's someone here to stay with him."

Ralph chortled. "Wouldn't be that pretty

little gal I saw on your porch when I drove in, would it?"

"She's a…tenant. Helps out in exchange for staying here."

This time, Ralph laughed out loud. "So that's what you young bucks call it these days."

Ethan could well imagine Abby's reaction if Ralph teased her about this. "Uh, Ralph—"

He waved away Ethan's concern. "Don't worry. I won't bring it up. I'd hate to perturb the young lady and leave you high and dry—"

"Ralph." Ethan tipped his head toward the doorway of the cabin, where Abby stood with an armload of sheets and towels. "Hi, Abby. Come on in."

She nodded politely to both of them as she stepped just inside the door. A faint blush stained her cheeks. "I expect you'll need these?"

"I surely do." With a devilish gleam in his eyes, Ralph took the linens from her. "I don't believe we've met, Miss—?"

Ethan quickly made the introductions and then headed out the door with his hand at the small of Abby's rigid back. He waited until they were well out of hearing range of the cabin. "You'll have to excuse Ralph. He's been widowed for years and he's quite an old coot, but he means no harm."

"Oh, I'm glad to be part of any risqué jokes around here. Believe me."

"I'm sorry, Abby. It won't happen again." He looked over at her, expecting to see her eyes flashing in anger.

Instead, she bumped his good arm with her shoulder and laughed. "This was nothing. You wouldn't believe the gossip chain at the hospital, or what people are saying about me living here. Not that it's their business."

"Then I'm sorry about that, too."

"I suppose it's because I'm new in the area and have a managerial position. Easy target. Ironic, isn't it? As far as the gossips are concerned I'm the wanton woman of the woods—and, here I am, leading the life of a nun."

But I'm so glad you're here. The thought came out of nowhere and hit him with the force of a speeding truck.

The truth of it hit him just as hard.

He'd promised her a safe place to live. She'd made her disinterest clear. And now he was sharing his house with a woman he just might be falling for.

The next seven weeks were going to be rough.

ON THURSDAY MORNING the weekly staff meeting at Ollie's was canceled in favor of a meeting with the committee heads of the hospital's dinner dance and silent auction fundraiser. So far, only Abby and Dr. Edwards had arrived at the conference room in the hospital, though the others were expected at any minute.

Jill leaned against one of the large round tables and folded her arms. "How's it going?"

Abby looked up from the stack of papers she was counting out and placing in front of each chair. "Regarding…?"

"The situation Leland mentioned a couple weeks ago."

"I haven't worked a clinical shift since then, so I haven't been involved in direct patient care." Distributing the last of the handouts, Abby glanced at the open doorway and lowered her voice. "No harm came from what happened with my charting, thank God, but I did remind the nurses that tampering with documentation is grounds for immediate dismissal. Perhaps even a formal reprimand or loss of state licensure. I would certainly pursue it to the fullest extent."

"Good. Has there been any more trouble?"

"Not that we've found." Abby glanced around the room. "But knowing that someone tried to frame me is more than a little frightening."

"Why would anyone do that? Could it have just been inadvertent?"

"I wish I could believe it was. But someone had to physically remove those assessments from the charts in the E.R. And there's no way altering progress notes could be accidental. Every nurse and aide knows documentation is inviolable. It's why we all use black, waterproof ink—mandated by administration and stated in the policy manual."

"Then back to my question. Why would anyone—"

Gwen and Carl, representing the nursing staff, walked in the door, followed by Marge from the business office, Erin Reynolds and Dr. Leland Anderson. By the time they were settled at the table, Dr. Connor Reynolds appeared, trailed by Leo Crupper, a local businessman who'd been on the hospital board for years.

"We're going to keep this to a half hour," Erin announced from the front of the room. "I know you're all busy, and we've had these plans set up for some time. I just want to make sure we're ready for the fundraiser next week. We don't want any surprises."

Leo stood and nodded to the others. "The food committee has the menu all set. We've got the hospital kitchen staff preparing the buffet, and we've got a nice cake donated by Ellen's Bakery—a big fancy one. The M & B Liquor store donated two cases of champagne. No new problems that I can see at this point."

Erin nodded and Leo sat. "Good news. Decorations?"

Carl scowled and nudged Gwen's arm, and settled deeper in his chair.

Obviously nervous about speaking in front of the others, Gwen stood and twisted her fingers together, her gaze fastened on the table in front of her. "Um…the Floral Experience promised a big bouquet for the head table and a single rose with fern in a crystal vase for each of the smaller ones. They suggested a raffle for the decorations, which will bring in more money."

"Great. Thanks." Erin jotted a few notes and then searched the room. "Music—that would be you, Dr. Anderson."

"All set. As you know, last month, my wife lined up the five-piece orchestra that played for our son's wedding. They're still on and have agreed to donate their services from nine until eleven that night." He smiled thinly. "Since I have two daughters getting married next year and I head up the entertainment committee at our club, they probably figured it's a smart investment."

Erin laughed. "Good for you, Leland. Marge?"

The older woman lumbered to her feet. "The silent auction plans are on schedule. We've got forty donations so far, ranging from home cleaning services to weekends at time-shares in Florida, Denver and the Bahamas, and the online bids are already starting to climb on those."

"And what about the car?"

"Fantastic. The bids are already up to seven thousand, and we've still got nine days to go. A lot of people are probably holding back until the night of the dinner, hoping they'll get a good deal."

"Thanks, Marge." Erin flipped to another page in her notebook. "We've got volunteers canvassing the county, selling tickets. So far, they've sold over three hundred for the dinner dance. At twenty dollars each, that's…"

Leo snorted. "Now where in creation are you gonna put three hundred people, much less feed 'em? I thought there was going to be a cap of two seventy-five."

"The pavilion at the county fairgrounds should still work fine," Erin said. "There've been wedding dances out there with four hundred guests. But not everybody will show up. There's a place on the ticket to mark if the purchase is just a donation rather than a plan to attend, and there've been about twenty of those so far." She looked around the room. "Any questions?"

Carl frowned at the clock and shifted in his chair. "I need to get back to the unit."

Abby watched him head for the door. She caught Jill watching him go, as well, her mouth pursed. Their eyes met.

Carl?

He was a highly competent nurse, but

he'd pulled a lot of sick time over the past six months and his veiled, sarcastic attitude had recently ruffled feathers at the hospital more than once.

Marcia had actually asked to change her shift so she wouldn't have to work with him again.

Could he be the one who'd tried to discredit Abby? But *why*?

CHAPTER FOURTEEN

ABBY PUNCHED HER PILLOW. Rolled over. Pulled the top sheet up to her chin. Then gave up trying to sleep entirely after a full night of tossing and turning.

Work was stressful, but she'd learned to expect that despite her initial misconception about quiet, small town hospitals.

So far, she had yet to take a single coffee break and she'd worked through most of her lunch breaks, as well.

On a positive note, on Monday she'd interviewed two enthusiastic young nurses from Madison with relatives in this area, so they'd be likely to stay long term.

Except neither could start for at least another two weeks.

But living here at Ethan's was proving to be difficult, as well.

She was gone during the day; he was gone every evening and most of the weekends.

When she saw him, he was elegantly polite. Friendly, but reserved.

He was, she'd discovered, an intelligent and witty man who was far more than just a handsome face.

At the sound of a key in the back door she grabbed her robe, cinched it tight and leaned against the door frame of her bedroom to watch him come in. "Hi."

He shucked off his boots and turned, surprise lighting his weary face. "You're up late. How come?"

"Couldn't sleep." She lifted a shoulder, wondering if she dared ask the question that had been on the tip of her tongue all week. "Things at work, I guess."

"Not going well?"

"Just…busy. The usual, plus the last-minute preparations for the dinner dance and silent auction this Saturday. If it goes well enough, we'll be able to replace a lot of the outdated equipment in the E.R."

"I read about it in the paper. Good cause." He opened the refrigerator and looked inside, then shut the door and touched the side of the coffeepot on the counter.

"It's still warm, but it's decaf. If you want

some chocolate-chip cookies, Keifer and I baked them tonight before he went to bed."

Ethan retrieved several from the cookie jar, poured himself a cup and turned to face her. "You've been wonderful for him. I don't know if I've thanked you for how you've taken over things around here."

"You have. Just about every day." She smiled, then took a deep breath. "So now I have a favor to ask you."

"Shoot."

"Frankly, I need a date for Saturday night, or I'm going to be dodging Leo Crupper and one of the retired doctors most of the night. You don't have to appear romantic," she added hastily when he raised a brow. "You don't even have to dance, but if you're there, I can tactfully fend them off."

Ethan chuckled. "Fend them off?"

"I'm just not in the market for a relationship with someone a good forty years older than I am."

"Sounds like fun," he said dryly. "But I couldn't leave Keifer alone, and that would be a long night."

"Erin offered to invite him to a sleepover

with her kids on Saturday. She's got a dependable babysitter."

"I can talk to Keifer and see what he thinks." Ethan hesitated. "You do know this would give the gossips more fuel if you and I arrive together."

"They haven't needed any. I hear I'm still quite the topic at the water cooler. Long after I leave town, I'll be remembered as that floozy from Detroit."

He laughed. The deep rich sound of it rolled over her.

"Then again, perhaps this isn't such a good idea. Maybe you've got your eye on somebody in town, and she could get the wrong idea."

"If that were the case, I think the horse is already out of the barn," he said with a smile. "But I'm not too concerned."

She fingered the collar of her robe. "This whole arrangement *was* your idea."

"That it was."

"I promise, I've never led anyone to believe there's anything going on between us."

"I haven't had any doubt on that score. Believe me." The laugh lines at the corners of his eyes deepened. "And if Keifer is comfortable about an overnight at Erin's, I'd be honored to go with you."

"Thanks. I—" A faint, keening sound rose outside the back door. "Is that Rufus?"

"Shouldn't be. I close her and the pups in the shed every night so they can't wander off."

They heard the eerie sound again, and she was suddenly very glad Ethan was here. "Maybe it's the wind."

He flipped on the porch light and looked outside. "Well, I'll be."

He pushed open the screen door, knelt and held out his hand. "C'mon, old girl, I'll bet someone here will be really glad to see you."

Belle.

Though from her muddy and bedraggled coat, it was hard to tell. She took one wary step forward. Then another, gingerly moving each paw. She'd been gaunt before, but now her ribs showed through her hide like the bars of an old-fashioned radiator, and her eyes were sunken. With each faltering step she left a smear of blood on the floor.

"Oh, my God," Abby breathed. "What happened to her?"

"Nothing good," Ethan growled. He grabbed

a cereal bowl from the cupboard, filled it with water and put in front of her.

She licked it dry and looked up at him, pleading for more.

"In a while, girl, or it'll come back up." He frowned as he headed out the back door. "I'll go get some of Rufus's dog food from the shed."

Abby pulled the entryway rug over and coaxed Belle onto it. The dog gingerly dropped down, her head on her extended front paws. The pads of her feet were worn raw and cut, as if she'd traveled a great distance. The skin and hair had been rubbed away over the angles of her hips and shoulders.

Abby ran a gentle hand over the dog's head and neck. "Why did you run away?"

Her fingers hit something sticky, wet. Belle flinched.

"Look at this," she whispered as Ethan came back inside. "It's awful."

A band of raw, abraded skin encircled the dog's neck, weeping blood where the wounds went deep.

Ethan swore under his breath. "Looks like someone tied her with a rope…maybe even dragged her behind a car. Call the sheriff, will you? We're going to report this right now, and we'll take her to a vet first thing in the morning."

She made the call, dialing with shaky fingers, then took a deep breath and turned back to Ethan and Belle.

He was on the floor, cradling the dog's head in his lap, crooning to her so softly, Abby could barely hear. When Abby came closer he looked up at her with anger blazing in his eyes.

"Whoever did this is dangerous, Abby. I wonder if he unlocked the gate and stole her. If I'm right, he's caused trouble here before and he could decide to come back. Maybe you'd better find a safer place to stay."

THE NEXT MORNING Abby called the hospital to tell them she'd be a few hours late, then she followed Ethan and Keifer into town. The vet examined and x-rayed Belle, cleansed her wounds and discovered she had areas of blunt trauma—possibly from being kicked, given the shape and size of them—and an abscess. They left the clinic with ten days of sulfa pills, antibiotic cream and directions to bring her back if she wasn't eating or drinking well.

At the sheriff's office, the deputy came outside to take a look at her.

"Unbelievable," Milt concluded as he ran a hand over the knobs of Belle's spine. "We see cruelty from time to time, and I always wonder why on earth anyone would treat an animal like this."

Ethan waited until Keifer wandered over to stare at a gleaming, chrome-encrusted Harley parked a few parking spaces down, then lowered his voice and recounted the incident with the damaged padlocks and his suspicions about the trio of young men he'd seen at the street dance. "I wanted to talk to them, but they saw me coming and disappeared."

Milt snorted. "Those three are trouble, and they're slippery. We found a portable meth lab last fall and we're almost sure they were involved, but they didn't leave prints and their daddies all had good alibis for 'em. Bobby Haskins's dad is the local bank president, and he was outraged that we'd even question the character of his son. Buford and Rowley claimed they were up north fishing with their boys that weekend."

Abby frowned. "Can you at least check into this? Talk to these people?"

"I'll talk to Sheriff Johnson. Maybe we can go out together and visit each of the families. But without proof..." He raised a brow and looked from Abby to Ethan. "Well, we won't have much to go on. Maybe your dog just wandered off and got tangled up in something and couldn't get free." Milt seemed to warm to the idea. "If an animal struggles long enough, it can sure do itself harm."

"I have trouble imagining that," Abby said firmly. "Just look at her. The rope burn goes around her neck. I hardly think she could've found a noose and put her head through it."

"It could also be someone else entirely. There's more'n a few farmers and townsfolk around here who've lost livestock and pets these past couple years." Milt chewed on his fleshy lower lip as he regarded Ethan. "A lot of 'em blame the wolves, and you've been real vocal about the repopulation program. Maybe there were cases you investigated. If someone didn't get his money, he might've been nursing a grudge ever since."

"I was fair, but I never authorized *unsubstantiated* wolf depredation claims." Ethan turned to Abby. "The state gives compensation for a verified wolf kill, but coyotes, bears and feral dogs kill, too."

"How can you tell which one did it?"

"We look for wolf tracks, scat or hair left at the site, teeth marks and method. The attack styles are very different. In one case, I just found tufts of hair and the owner seemed nervous. The sheriff and I figured the animal had been stolen or secretly sold, but we could never prove it."

"That might be," the deputy said, "but folks around here get pretty tense about these things, whether there's proof or not."

Ethan nodded, ignoring the warning in the deputy's tone. "That's true. But you know as well as I do, there's always someone trying to abuse the system, no matter what the situation."

"Right." Apparently mollified, the deputy adjusted his service belt and gave Belle a final glance before turning to go back into the building. "I'll let you know what the sheriff and I find out."

Abby waited until he disappeared inside. "He sure didn't seem very concerned."

"One sheriff and two part-time deputies cover the whole county. They've got a lot on their plate already, and a case like this is hard to solve and hard to bring to court. It might be different if we'd caught a license plate or had a witness."

"So he won't do anything." She tried and failed to rein in the bitterness in her voice. "It doesn't matter?"

"It matters. Anyone who'd mistreat an animal like this isn't normal, Abby. Maybe he got a kick out of it. And if he did this as some sort of retaliation, it could escalate and he could come back for even bigger stakes."

She shivered, thinking about the many miles between Ethan's house and the nearest neighbors. The deep, dark woods surrounding his place, and the vast government land beyond it to the north.

"I can only hope that next time, I'll be there to get him." Ethan glanced protectively at Keifer, who was still eyeing the motorcycle. His voice turned soft. Deadly. "Because no one is going to threaten my family, livestock or me and get away with it."

ETHAN HAD ENCOURAGED Abby to move to a safer place in town, and she'd thought about it. Carefully.

But she'd said she'd stay. There were, after all, good locks on the doors. There was a steady stream of fishermen renting the two cabins, and they were within calling distance during the night.

Besides, she really had nowhere else to go.

Hooking a crystal chandelier earring into place, she went to the living room doorway. "So, are you packed for your overnight?" she asked. "We need to leave in a few minutes."

Keifer slumped lower in the sofa and didn't look up from the video game he was playing. "I don't *want* to."

"You've met the Reynolds kids in town. Remember? We saw them in the grocery store. Twice."

No answer.

"I know those kids, and I promise you, you're going to have lots of fun."

He stared at the screen.

"The thing is, this is a great chance to get to know them. They like video games, too, and they're…" She thought back to the night she'd had them all over at her apartment in Hubert's house. "*Very* energetic."

Abby glanced nervously at her watch. Ethan had returned from fishing an hour later than he'd expected, after having some sort of problems with his boat's motor. He'd disappeared into his room, tired and drawn, and she'd been anxiously pacing ever since.

Though she'd helped with the decorations out at the pavilion until almost one o'clock this morning, there were still last-minute preparations, and they needed to drop Keifer at Erin's house first.

On the verge of asking Keifer to go in and check on his dad, she looked over to see Ethan standing in the door of his bedroom.

Her breath caught in her throat. *Oh, my.*

In a perfectly cut black blazer and crisp charcoal pants, with a black shirt and a burgundy tie, he looked as sophisticated as any city guy heading to an art gallery.

Finally remembering to breathe, she reached for her silver-beaded evening bag. "You look wonderful," she told him.

He looked her over slowly, head to toe. "Very, very nice. Red is definitely your color."

Red, actually, had been her only color, as this was the only dressy outfit she'd packed for the summer. Why on earth had she brought this one?

She tugged at the scooped neckline—which

dropped lower in the back—and wished the hemline was a few inches longer. "I sure hope this is appropriate for Blackberry Hill. If not—" she grabbed her lacy black shawl from the back of the sofa "—then I'll be swathed in this thing the entire evening."

Ethan's appreciative grin widened. "Let's hope not. I'd sure like to see what those elderly beaus of yours do when they see you. They might just trample me."

Now that she'd seen Ethan, she realized fending off the old folks might have been a better choice.

"We'd better get going," he said, his gaze lingering on her.

"You're right." She shouldered the delicate strap of her purse. "We'll, um, be lucky if we make it to the fairgrounds by five."

Keifer grumbled as he grabbed his backpack and went out onto the porch.

Abby started to follow, but Ethan touched her arm. She glanced up at him, prepared for one more reminder that she should think about moving back to town, but then their eyes met and the intensity of his gaze sent a shiver through her.

With just a half step toward him, she knew

she'd be walking right into his arms…and moving into a situation she wasn't ready to handle.

Especially not with a ten-year-old boy pacing the porch.

"You look stunning tonight, Abby." His voice was low, and a faint smile played at the corners of his mouth.

And just like that, the careful distance they'd maintained seemed to melt away like ice cream on a hot summer's day.

"There's just something about red sequins…or is it those shoes?" he added. "Must be the shoes."

He dropped a swift kiss on her mouth, then lifted her chin with a forefinger. "You are going to drive those old guys wild."

CHAPTER FIFTEEN

THE PAVILION at the fairgrounds was a huge red-brick building with black-and-white tiled floors, white walls and a stage at one end. Come country fair time it would be filled with tables of 4-H exhibits and clusters of chairs where the youngsters demonstrated their projects.

This evening it was a magical place, transformed with swags of black, white and mauve chiffon. A hundred cloth-draped tables had been set with silver-rimmed white china and crystal donated by the local party supplier. The colors in the massive centerpiece of Peace roses, baby's breath, fern and purple iris on the head table were repeated in perfect, single roses on the other tables.

Ethan touched Abby's shoulder and strolled across the room to talk to Peter Barton, the owner of the feed supply store, while she stopped at each table to check the place settings.

Instead of the long banks of bright fluorescent lights overhead, flickering candles at each table provided soft illumination. Last night she'd helped the volunteers fold each napkin into an upright tulip tied with a mauve satin bow, and dressed each chair in a mauve linen cover tied at the back with a snowy tulle bow.

The little napkin soldiers were all still standing at attention, thank goodness, and the silverware gleamed in the candlelight. *Perfect*.

"You've all absolutely outdone yourselves!"

Abby turned to discover Grace at her side. The older woman was dressed in a fuchsia full-length dress topped with a mint-fuchsia-and-black floral jacket that flattered her stocky figure. The glittery peacock brooch on her jacket didn't begin to match the sparkle in her eyes.

Abby gave the hospital's retired director of nursing a swift hug. "Amazing, isn't it? We've already grossed almost nine thousand on the meal and dance alone."

"The donor list is impressive." Grace waved one of the brochures she'd picked up by the door. "The volunteers have done a fantastic job."

"And the silent auction, have you taken a good look?" Abby nodded toward the tables along the back wall, where gift baskets, merchandise and posters advertised the items being offered.

One piece, a crystal sculpture of a howling wolf with a pup at its side, was so exquisite in its detail—Abby couldn't believe someone would donate such a treasure. And at the end of the table, a large color poster displayed the crowning item: a restored, candy-apple-red 1966 Mustang donated by three area car dealers.

"The car alone is already up to almost eight thousand," Abby marveled. "This should be an exciting night!"

Grace smiled. "Thanks to you and the others who've worked so hard. I'm afraid I haven't been any help at all."

"You had Erin's boys for a while, though, and I hear you've done more traveling since then. Was it Washington, D.C.?"

"A couple weeks out east. Since then we've been busy wallpapering and painting."

Abby bit her lower lip and glanced around the near-empty room. "I'd like to talk to you sometime. Privately, if I could. About something that happened at the hospital."

"Of course." Grace's eyebrows drew together. "Is there something wrong?"

So Dr. Anderson hadn't reported the charting situation to her, then. He and Grace went back so far in their association at the hospital that Abby had figured he might have. She glanced around once more and lowered her voice. "I've had a problem with someone. I think it's one of the nurses, though I can't identify who. I thought you might have some ideas."

The furrow in Grace's brow deepened. She took a piece of paper and a pen from her evening bag, jotted down her name and number, and handed it to Abby. "We can certainly discuss it, though I honestly never had a lick of serious trouble with any of the staff at the hospital now. But do call me tomorrow."

"Thanks."

A distinguished, elderly gentleman waved to Grace from the silent auction display. "That's Warren," she said fondly. "I'd better see what he's up to."

"And I'd better see if Erin needs anything done." Abby laughed. "I've been her administrative assistant for this affair, but she's so efficient I haven't had much to do."

She found Erin in the entryway of the pavilion, her face flushed and her eyes wild. A hospital van had been backed up to the wide double doors. "They're here *early*," she moaned. "And of all things, we've got parmesan-crusted chicken breasts. We can't keep them warm here—and if we send them back, they'll be overdone and dried out in another two hours. Chicken is so fragile."

The recently hired manager of the dietary department, Georgia Yancey, pulled herself up, clearly in a snit. "We were *told* five o'clock. And it wasn't easy, preparing all of this while taking care of the patient and staff meals at the same time."

"But the flyers have been all over town.

In the hallways at the hospital. There were several articles in the paper."

"Mr. Crupper specifically said five o'clock," Georgia repeated. "He called just this week, to make sure everything was in order."

Erin turned to Abby. "Leo must have gotten it mixed up," she said grimly. "Five o'clock was the time for us to be here for the last-minute preparations. Not *dinner*. Where is Leo, anyway?"

"I haven't seen him." Abby stared at the banks of stainless-steel containers in the truck. "What are our best options, Georgia?"

"Start over."

"Okay, then—what options can we afford?" Abby thought fast. "You've had a number of years experience in a Chicago country club, right? What about putting the chicken directly on the wild rice, instead of having them separate, and then covering it all with some sort of white wine sauce?"

"I could do that, sure. Menu won't match what we advertised."

"At this point, we need edible. Memorable. Not a perfect match."

"I'll seal it in foil, then, while it's being held. With plenty of the sauce, low heat. A touch of bacon, sautéed mushrooms, maybe." Georgia pursed her lips. "Caramelized onions as a garnish?"

"Wow. I think I should come along and help you taste test. You're even making junior hungry." Erin grinned and patted her round belly. "People should actually be coming well before seven to bid on the silent auction. Maybe we can serve earlier, if they're all here?"

Georgia's eyes opened wider. "The servers. Oh, man—they're already on their way." She scurried out to her van, flung open the driver's side door and lunged inside for her cell phone.

After a few minutes of animated conversation she rounded the back of the truck, closed the doors and drove off.

"Leo was head of the food committee, but he should have gone through me for anything involving hospital staff." Erin watched the van disappear. "I'm going to personally kill him. The minute that man walks in the building, he is *history*. What else can go wrong?"

"Nothing. It's a perfect summer evening. The decorations are lovely." A group of men in tuxes appeared at the door carrying instrument cases and music stands. "And with the orchestra here, we should be set. Best of all, I saw the hospital's maintenance crew out here this afternoon, spraying for mosquitoes."

"Thank heavens." Erin's face lit up. "That reminds me, believe it or not, of something I've been meaning to ask you."

"Fire away."

"The surgeon in Chicago was really positive about correcting Lily's clubfoot, and he has a sterling reputation. Lily is so thrilled.… Yesterday we got a letter saying he has an opening in his surgery schedule the last week in August."

"Will you take it?"

"Absolutely. Lily has been beaming ever since. She'd hoped to be just like the other kids when school starts again." Erin smiled. "She's such a little trouper. She knows she'll have a cast and crutches for the first few weeks of school, but she doesn't want to wait a moment longer."

"Wonderful news." Abby gave her friend a quick hug. "Do you want me to watch the boys again?"

Erin regarded her doubtfully. "They got you evicted last time, and this would be for five or six days."

"Keifer will be back in Minneapolis by then, but I'll still be in town that last week. I'll check with Ethan."

"I can't thank you enough. I figured it might be too much for Grace and Warren again, and none of our relatives live anywhere close."

"Just curious, though—how in the world did mosquitoes remind you of this?"

Erin made a face. "Yesterday evening the boys took Lily outside to play catch, *without* bug spray. All three came back covered with bites—especially Lily. Connor told her it's because she's such a sweet girl, but she moves a lot slower than the other two, so she's probably an easier target."

"Poor baby."

"I owe you, after this." Erin touched Abby's hand in gratitude. "Oh, look, people are already coming!"

They stood and watched as couples started strolling into the building; a rainbow of pretty dresses contrasting with the dark suits and blazers. People Abby recognized from businesses in town and from church. Hospital board members and their spouses. Staff members including Gwen, who arrived with several of the other nurses, and Carl, who'd arrived with one of the nurse's aides.

Dr. Edwards walked in arm-in-arm with her husband, Grant. Her long skirt and loose, silver-sequined halter top masked the curve of her five-month pregnancy, although the attentiveness and obvious adoration in Grant's eyes still gave it away.

Gwen waved, then stopped next to Abby. "This is going to be a wonderful night for the hospital, isn't it?"

"I'm just hoping it all goes well."

"I've been meaning to ask you about your new dog." Gwen touched a rhinestone poodle brooch pinned to her filmy emerald dress. "A friend mentioned that you'd gotten one, and I just wanted to tell you about the obedience classes at the high school every fall. What kind of dog did you get?"

"A mix, probably some springer and golden retriever. She's too shy for crowds, though."

"Really." Gwen regarded her thoughtfully. "That'll change if you take her to the lessons. They sure helped my Petey." She rose up on her tiptoes and waved to someone across the room. "Oops, there's my daughter. I'd better get over there before she buys everything in sight."

She crossed the room and disappeared into the crowd around the Mustang display.

Ethan broke away from a conversation and sauntered toward Abby.

Easily a head taller than most of the other men, his confident, easy grace set him apart from the others.

"He looks like he really wants something. Probably *you*." Erin gave Abby a nudge and a wink. "Now, tell me that man isn't interested. Just look at the gleam in his eyes!" She feigned an exaggerated glance at her wrist. "Oops, I think I need to check on...something. I'll leave you kids to yourselves."

"So," Abby said crisply, waving a hand to encompass the pavilion and the people. "What do you think?"

Ethan's left dimple deepened. "That you're easily the most beautiful woman here. That your dress is...amazing."

"Spandex and sequins. I look forward to being able to breathe in about five hours."

He moved closer and rested a possessive hand at her waist. "Of course, you're awfully cute in jeans and a tee, too."

Out of the corner of her eye she saw Dr. Ericksson hovering not more than fifteen feet away, and realized why Ethan had moved so close. "Thanks. I'm sure he got the message this time."

"Who?"

"You are definitely my white knight. Keep it up and I'll make breakfast tomorrow—even if it isn't part of our deal." She tipped her head toward the silent auction tables and looped her arm through his. "Let's go take a look and see if there's anything you simply can't live without."

ANYTHING YOU CAN'T live without. That wouldn't be the trinkets and time-shares and electronic gizmos displayed so artfully between mounds of silvery gauze. But Abby...

Tonight she'd twisted her blond hair up into some sort of knot, with curly tendrils framing her face.

How it stayed in place was a mystery... but it *looked* as if unfastening that single bar of diamonds might release the entire thing and let all that silky hair cascade down her back.

He'd mostly tried to avoid looking.

If he wasn't careful, he was going to risk destroying the delicate balance they'd managed to achieve—camaraderie—with any sort of physical awareness held firmly in check.

"So, did you, um, have a nice visit with Peter?"

Another little tendril of hair had escaped its mooring and now hung provocatively at her cheek; a gleaming, curling ribbon of gold. It took him a second to remember who Peter was. "Uh...yeah."

She watched him expectantly, one delicately arched brow raised. "You two looked awfully intense. Is anything wrong?"

"Nothing that should interfere with tonight."

She frowned. "Okay, now you *have* to tell me. Is it something about your trespasser? Or Belle?"

A good question. "Peter sees a lot of local traffic at his store—farmers buying feed and seed, townsfolk coming for dog food. The guys hang around to drink coffee and play cards. He says there's been rising anger over some recent wolf kills. Given the location, it was probably the Lake Lunara pack."

A narrow line creased between her brows. "The one you've been studying."

"Right. Two kills were verified and the compensation forms have been submitted. It's illegal to hunt the wolves, but there's talk about someone needing to take care of the problem, once and for all."

"Did he catch any names?"

"None of them were stupid enough to say *they'd* do it. The state pays fair market value. But they're saying that reparation doesn't begin to cover the years of cultivating good breeding stock, or the emotional attachment if a pet is lost."

"I guess I understand that, but it's still illegal to hunt wolves, right?"

"To the tune of some hefty fines."

"*If* the guy is caught."

"But thousands of acres of timber, wetlands and the sparse population up here make that a tough job." Ethan shook his head slowly. "Catching a single poacher in Northern Wisconsin is about as easy as finding a lost contact lens in a lake, unless someone calls in a tip."

An image of the Lunara pack's alpha female playing with her pups flashed through his thoughts. Last year she'd whelped four and successfully raised two. Both had been with the pack this summer as yearlings, though come October, they'd likely disperse perhaps seventy miles or more to establish their own territories.

One of them wouldn't be making that trip.

"Frank Carter is the interim wolf biologist for this area. He called me this afternoon, and said there's a mortality signal coming from a radio collar in the Lunara area."

"That doesn't sound good."

"It isn't. The collar has been still for too long. Occasionally a wolf can slip a collar, but it usually means the wolf is dead."

THE DINNER—despite Leo's interference—came off without a hitch. The spinach, strawberry and mandarin salads were topped with a zippy raspberry vinaigrette dressing, the chicken was moist and tender on its bed of wild rice.

Georgia hadn't been able to salvage the broccoli, which had turned olive-drab and had to be pitched, but the second batch was bright green, al dente and perfect.

And even better than the decadent cappuccino mousse swirled into edible chocolate cups for dessert, the orchestra was innovative and Ethan, by all accounts, proved to be a superb dancer.

That meant Abby ended up giving him to the bank president's wife, Erin and to several other women who'd practically wrenched him away for the privilege of a dance.

"I'm back, and I'm not leaving," he said, grinning down at her as he led Abby through an intricate salsa. "If one of those other women come back, feel free to belt them."

"No way. You can get arrested for assault, not me." She stumbled slightly but he held her securely. "Oops, sorry. I don't think I've done this one since college. Where did you learn to dance so well?"

"My ex-wife. She was a dance instructor when we were in college."

"Very private lessons," Abby teased.

"Much needed, but not all that successful," he said with a wry grin. "She said I was one of her least adept students. Ever."

Appalled, Abby pulled back to look up at him. "I hope you didn't believe her."

The music changed. Smooth, powerful and confident, he spun her into a graceful waltz that left her breathless and laughing, almost too dizzy to stand when the music faded away.

From the perimeter of the room she heard a

round of applause and opened her eyes to see that she and Ethan were alone in the center of the dance floor.

"Oh!" Embarrassed, she tried to leave, but his large hand encircled her wrist and held her securely.

He nodded to the onlookers, encouraging them back onto the floor as the orchestra segued into a timeless, romantic rendition of "Unforgettable," perfect for slow, slow dancing.

And as if they'd done it a thousand times, she stepped into his arms, leaned her head against his chest and listened to the strong and steady beat of his heart. This time they barely moved, just swayed and turned to the deeply emotional music.

When it ended, she looked up and what she saw in his gaze made her breath catch in her throat. "We're all right together, aye?" he murmured, too low for anyone else to hear.

She smiled at the colloquial northern Minnesota phrasing that had slipped into his speech. "We are. But this was just about dancing. Poignant music. Nothing more than that."

But it wasn't.

If she wasn't careful, he'd be the man who held her heart in his gentle hand, long after she'd left Blackberry Hill.

CHAPTER SIXTEEN

BY MIDNIGHT, the silent auction had netted almost sixteen thousand dollars, and the partygoers had all left. The inside of the pavilion was in shambles.

"We can lock up the building and do the rest of the cleanup tomorrow," Erin said wearily. "It's been a long couple of days."

"If enough volunteers show up, it should go pretty fast." Abby drummed her fingers on the cash box sitting on the head table, then tapped the stack of silent auction sheets into a neat pile. "Tonight we just need to get the money to the hospital safe. On Monday we can count it and compare it to the receipts before it all goes to the bank."

"We can take it," Erin said. But there were dark circles under her eyes and she swayed on her feet.

"You look as if you're ready to fall over,"

Abby protested. "I'd be happy to drop it off. Just tell me where to put it."

"There's a safe in the main office, but even I don't remember that combination." She thought for a moment. "There's a smaller one in my office, though. It should be fine, since my office is locked. Sure you don't mind?"

"No problem."

Erin gave her a smile of pure gratitude. "I'll drop by tomorrow and move the money to the main safe." She reached for a ring of keys inside her purse, twisted one off and handed it to Abby. "This key gets you into my office. The safe combination is on the inside back cover of the old pharmacology textbook on top of my file cabinet. The numbers," she added with a wink, "are written backward."

"Sounds secure to me."

After a round of farewells, Leo locked the pavilion doors and soon a stream of taillights headed out to the highway.

Moaning with relief, Abby kicked off her heels and curled her toes against the carpeting in Ethan's pickup. "Nothing could feel better than getting these off."

"You must be worn out." He looked down at the standard transmission stick shift. "If that wasn't in the way, I'd tell you to move close so you could sleep against my shoulder."

"It'll only take a few minutes in the hospital. After that it won't be long till we're home."

She leaned against the headrest and turned her head to study his profile. Illuminated by the dashboard lights, his square jaw and strong, high cheekbones were thrown into sharp relief. "Thanks for a wonderful evening."

His smile deepened the vertical creases bracketing his mouth. "You're the one to thank, not me. I just came along for the ride, but you've been working on this for a long time."

"You made it fun, though. For a recluse, you can be a pretty social guy."

He laughed. *"Recluse?"*

"Half the people at the dance didn't seem to even recognize you."

"The country club set wouldn't. I haven't golfed since college, and I've never cared much for small talk with people I barely know."

"So what's in your future? I know you're studying the wolf pack. But what then?"

"I'm halfway through my year of sabbatical. I'll compile my notes, work on my photographs and text and hopefully see my book in print. After that? I'll either go back to working for the Wisconsin DNR or look into teaching environmental sciences at a college. I had an offer from River Falls a while back." He slid a look at her. "Not anything like what you're heading for, princess. Bright lights, big city? That would drive me over the edge."

"Princess?"

"Honey, you might wear jeans and sneakers most of the time and you might be working for a small-town hospital, but you have Old Money written all over you."

It was her turn to laugh. "Maybe, but I'll sure never see it. My dad loved being a philosophy prof at a small college out east, even though it didn't pay well. And later, he and my mother lost most of their investments during stock downturns."

"Yet you followed suit, with teaching?"

"The money doesn't matter. I love teaching and the whole atmosphere of academia. The start of school in the fall, with a new wave of students. The smell of books and the world of the arts that surrounds a college. The conversations over tea at coffeehouses on campus."

"You should like your new job in California, then."

"I'm sure I will." But watching the towering pines flashing by in the beams of the headlights, she wasn't really so sure anymore.

She thought she heard him sigh. "Still going on your Grand Tour, are you?"

"I've been planning it for a year. The most circuitous route you could imagine. From here to the Ozarks, then to the Enchanted Circle in New Mexico. Then up the spine of the Rockies through the Tetons and Glacier to Banff."

"Then Washington state and Oregon?"

Embarrassed, she dropped back in her seat. "Guess I mentioned it already."

"A few times. But hey, not many people dare follow their dreams."

"You sure have. I'd love to tag along someday, when you go out to study the wolf pack."

"Maybe early tomorrow morning, before I pick up Keifer at Erin's? I take him on hikes, but never very far. He gets too restless and bored."

"I'll plan on it. Thanks!"

At the hospital, Ethan pulled up to the front entrance. "Want me to come in?"

"This will just take a second." She slipped her shoes on, fumbled for her keys, and hopped out. "Be right back."

Inside, a single table lamp illuminated the empty reception area and waiting room. Beyond the carpeted area, polished flooring led to the long-term-care wing to the left, the hospital wing to the right, and ahead, to business administration.

The hallway was dim, but brighter aprons of light down the patient care wings marked the two nurses' stations. The silence was almost overwhelming as she hurried to Erin's office with the cash box and stack of auction receipts.

At Erin's office she dug into her purse for the key Erin had given her and unlocked the door, then reached inside for the light switch.

From behind her she heard a soft rustle. The squeak of a rubber-soled shoe.

And then something hit the back of her head with blinding force. Someone grabbed her...

She fell forward. Flailing her arms, she

tried to catch the edge of a chair…and landed on the carpet in a tangle of chair legs.

Her head throbbed. Her ankle hurt.

And behind her, she heard the soft *click* of a closing door.

MINUTES PASSED. Five, then ten.

Ethan considered the possibility that Abby was conferring with staff—maybe taking care of some problem—but an uneasy feeling settled in his gut when she still hadn't come out after fifteen minutes.

He launched out of the car and jogged to the Emergency entrance, where he ran into a startled nurse who gave him a quick head-to-toe glance, as if checking for obvious wounds or illness.

"Can I help you, sir?"

"Abby Cahill came in quite a while ago to drop something off, but she never came back outside."

The nurse frowned. "She hasn't been here all night."

"Not here in the E.R.—she went to the administrative wing." He brushed past her and started up the hall. "I'm going to check on her."

"Wait—you can't just go—"

"Call security. Have someone meet me there." He broke into a jog. Behind him, the nurse started to protest. "*Call* them."

A man in uniform arrived at the administrative hall just as Ethan turned the corner. "Joe Barker, head of security," he said sharply. "Visitors aren't allowed after hours."

The doors were closed on both sides of the hall. No sign of Abby anywhere. No sign of trouble. "I'm with Abby—or I was. I've been waiting for her in my truck, but she never came back out."

"She wouldn't be here this time of night. Now, if you don't mind…" Barker gestured toward the main entrance.

"She had a key to Erin's office," Ethan snapped. "She was dropping off the money from the silent auction. Now, which office is it?"

His hand hovering over the holster on his service belt, the man glowered suspiciously back at him. "One could guess that you're here hoping to *find* that money, so maybe we'd better have a little talk—"

From down the hall they heard a low moan.

"Abby? Abby!" Ethan shouldered past the

guard and tried several doorknobs before reaching a door with a small brass plaque engraved with Erin Reynolds. The knob twisted freely in his hand. He shoved the door open.

Abby sat on the floor of the office cupping the back of her head with her hand, her hair disheveled. One of the office chairs had tipped over. Papers were strewn everywhere.

She managed a weak smile. "Guess I had some unexpected company. Can someone call the police?"

SHERIFF JOHNSON ARRIVED ten minutes later. He and Joe conferred for a moment, then Joe left. The sheriff uncapped his pen. "I understand someone shoved you from behind. Correct?"

"With enough force that I landed on the floor." Abby sat at the edge of her chair, nervously twisting a tissue in her hands. She still felt cold, numb with shock, and she couldn't quite control her shaking hands.

He frowned as he surveyed her from head to foot. "Are you hurt?"

"No. Mostly surprised and scared. I might end up with a few bruises, but that's it." She scooped her tangled hair away from her face and pointed to the haphazard stack of papers on the desk. "I was carrying those papers and a small cash box containing personal checks, a cashier's check for eleven thousand on the auctioned car and almost five thousand in cash. The box is gone."

The sheriff walked through the room without touching anything. "Someone was in here waiting for you?"

"I think he was out in the hall and followed me."

He stopped, his pen poised over his clipboard. "You're sure it was a man?"

"No. I just assumed."

"Did he speak? Did you hear anything else?"

"No...well, maybe the squeak of a shoe. I was bringing in the proceeds from the fundraiser tonight. Who would've known that I'd be here, right at this time?" She shivered, remembering the people who'd been out at the pavilion until the very end. Erin and Connor. Jill and Grant. Leo Crupper, who was too small and wiry to do anyone much harm. A few of the elderly hospital volunteers—all gray-haired ladies hardly powerful enough to knock her over. "It can't have been a coincidence. How often would anyone carry that kind of money into this hospital?"

Ethan, who'd propped a hip on the edge of Erin's desk, cleared his throat. "She wasn't in here alone more than fifteen minutes. I was waiting outside and I didn't see anyone come or go."

Joe reappeared at the doorway. "I've talked to the staff on both wings, and no one has seen a soul tonight. The doors all buzz if someone tries to enter the building without a key at night…and on the long-term unit, the doors buzz if anyone tries to leave."

The sheriff asked Abby a series of questions while making notes. "We're going to search the building and question the staff more thoroughly, but you can go home for now."

Until this moment she'd felt numb, as if she'd been observing the past half hour from a distance. Now the reality started to sink in.

What if her attacker had used a weapon?

She shuddered. "I can't believe this happened. And you know what's ironic? We accepted just a few checks from impulse buyers. The top bidders on the car had to bring a cashier's check for their bid. But otherwise, our auction revenue was in cash. If we'd welcomed checks, then at least they could've been stopped."

BY THE TIME she stepped into Ethan's house, her whole body was shaking.

"You must be exhausted," Ethan said as he let Belle back into the house after a trip outside. "It's been one tough day."

"It was a wonderful day, till the end. Now, I keep remembering the squeaky shoe and being shoved into that dark office. I never had a chance to see who it was." Belle nudged Abby's hand with her nose. "At least I have my ferocious guard dog…and you."

"You'll be safe here, Abby. I'll make sure of it."

"Thank you."

He nodded as he locked the door, then moved from one window to the next and checked each lock.

"And thanks for everything else," she added. "Most of this night was very special… except when all those ladies kept stealing my dance partner. Oh, and when I got mugged. Minor points, really." His low laugh made her feel warmer, as if things might soon be normal again. "But I'd really like to end it on a different note, or there's no way I'll be able to sleep."

She took a deep breath and crossed the room, hoping he wouldn't embarrass her by refusing. When she reached him, she looked into his eyes for a long moment before he took her in his arms and held her tight, her head nestled below his chin. The steady beat of his heart reassured her as no words could have.

She was falling in love—and, unless she was mistaken, so was he.

She pulled away to look up at him and found in his eyes what she felt in her soul. And before he could back away, she curved a hand around his neck and pulled him close. *"Kiss me."*

And he did.

WAKING UP THE NEXT morning, Abby smiled to herself at the memory of the evening before, and she was eager to get up and see Ethan again. He had been so tender, so gentle with her when she'd needed comforting—and that simple kiss had felt more right than anything had in a long time.

But reality set in after the first cup of coffee, when he'd barely looked at her before going out to do chores, and hadn't even asked how she was feeling after getting hit on the head last night.

Given her plans to move away soon after Keifer left, that distance should have been reassuring. But instead it left her lonelier than she'd been in a long, long time. Bereft. And hurt. She knew he'd felt what she had last night, yet he could so easily throw it away.

"Very well," she said softly, staring out the kitchen window toward the trees as Ethan came into view. "That's how it will be."

And she certainly had far more pressing concerns, anyway. She'd called both the hospital and Erin the moment he went outside, but there'd been no news about the missing money or the person who'd assaulted her.

Her sore muscles and bruises didn't begin to compare with the awful image of the attack—and how much worse it might have been.

Shoving those thoughts aside, she bustled around the kitchen, straightening up, then pulled a pork roast out of the freezer, put it on a plate and set it in the refrigerator to start thawing for supper.

By the time Ethan walked in, she'd made her bed and started folding her laundry with her back to the open bedroom door.

She heard him hesitate at her door. "I need to go out into the timber," he said. "But I'll be back in time to go into town with you. I know you'll need help at the pavilion."

She turned, straightened and hit him with her breeziest smile. "Not at all. There'll be plenty of people there, so don't give it a second thought. In fact, I can pick up Keifer when I'm in town and save you the trip."

He blinked.

"One thing I'd like, though, is to hike to Lake Lunara, if that's where you're heading. After all, I've only got another four weeks before I leave."

"I know we talked about it, but I'm not sure this is a good time."

"Why not? It's a beautiful day. I actually thought about going by myself, but I'd feel safer with someone along."

A muscle ticked at the side of his jaw.

"This isn't really a pleasure trip, though. Frank Carter emailed this morning and asked if I could track down the wolf collar emitting a mortality signal."

"Isn't that his job?"

"It is, but I spend a great deal of time in that area anyway, and he's got another commitment."

"I'll just tag along, then. Honestly, I could really use a distraction."

"Of course." His frown faded. "Have you heard anything?"

"Not yet. I'm just hoping someone saw my attacker last night, and that the money turns up."

"I hope so, too." He glanced up at the clock. "If you really do want to come along, I'll have you back in time to leave for the fairgrounds."

"Super." He still didn't sound thrilled about her company, but that didn't matter. She lifted a pair of khaki shorts and a scarlet T-shirt out of the laundry basket. "Excuse me. I'll just be a minute."

She closed the door gently, suppressing the sudden urge to shut it in his face.

CHAPTER SEVENTEEN

ABBY WAS A CITY GIRL. A high heels, art museum and mocha latte kind of girl.

Until yesterday, she'd never said a word about wanting to go along on any adventuresome hikes. Maybe she'd really needed a distraction, but watching her striding on ahead of him, he wondered if she'd insisted on coming along today because she'd wanted to prove something.

He was crazy about her—and he'd almost said so last night. Today, he was trying to keep things under control. But it wasn't easy.

She'd actually come up with a serious pair of well-worn Montrail hiking boots, which surprised him. And she looked cute—too cute—with her hair in a bouncy ponytail pulled through the back of her ball cap.

He'd started out slow to accommodate her, but she'd given him a perky wave and struck out at a faster pace with the condescending promise that she'd wait up for him a mile or so down the trail.

If she'd gone fifty miles an hour he wouldn't have given her the satisfaction of putting distance between them, though her emotional distance was proving to be its own kind of punishment.

Every step reminded him of how sweet and beautiful and smart she was. Of how much he'd been enjoying her company this past month. And how foolish it had been to let her get close last night. He'd already known he was going to miss her, come September. Now he was going to miss her even more.

Gritting his teeth, he picked up his pace. "Veer to the right after that next big boulder," he called.

When he got there she'd propped herself against the boulder and was applying suntan lotion.

"Want some?" She replaced the cap and held out the plastic bottle. Her dark sunglasses and the bill of her cap shaded her eyes, but her teeth flashed white as she smiled. "It's SPF 50."

"No thanks." He gave her a wide berth.

"We need to keep moving, if we're to get home by noon."

"Right." She bounced to her feet and stowed the lotion in her pack. "How long do you figure this will take?"

"Three hours, easily. I can take you back, if this is too much for you," he suggested hopefully.

"Not at all." She flashed a smile. "You know, we uptown girls do our hiking on high heels and cement during all those shopping trips, so this is a snap."

Had he *said* something about her being incapable—or had he just thought it? Trying to remember, he caught the edge of his backpack against a poplar trunk and nearly lost his footing.

"Careful," she called.

He pushed on ahead, moving faster than he normally would. By the time he got over the next hill, he felt guilty. She'd been nothing more than pleasant and enthusiastic today.

A credit to her, given the stressful day yesterday. He was acting like a complete jerk.

And right now she was lagging behind, probably exhausted and developing blisters.

He turned to go back over the rise and nearly ran into her.

She held out her hand and fluttered her fingertips under his nose. "What do you think—is this too, too red?"

The pungent odor of wet nail polish assailed his nose. She was doing her *nails* while she walked?

She pulled them back and studied them. "Maybe so. But let's keep going, okay? I really would love to see that lake." She patted her fanny pack. "I've got a two-gig disk in my digital camera, so I can take *hundreds* of pictures."

"I'm not sure we'll have that kind of time."

"Not to worry. I can pretty much take them on the run," she chirped. "I wouldn't dream of being an inconvenience."

Realization hit him like a fast ball to the gut. "This is about last night," he said. "Between you and me."

"Last night?" She bit her lip, looking truly mystified. "I have no idea what you mean."

He needed to tread softly here. If she broke down and got all emotional, how would he get her all the way back home? And *when?* Barbara had always wanted to talk, too. And talk and talk and talk. Especially when she was upset. Which is how, on one fateful night, he'd unexpectedly found himself engaged to the last woman on earth he ever should have married.

"You're upset with me," he said carefully.

She gave a noncommittal shrug. "Why?"

"Something happened between us last night, and this morning I…backed away."

An airy flip of her hand dismissed his concern. "Let's just drop the subject, okay?"

He'd woken up this morning dreading any long-term expectations she might have after the romance of the dance and their good-night kiss. Now he was free and clear…though he wasn't too sure he was happy about it.

If she wasn't upset over that, maybe he'd looked too dubious when she'd hauled out those serious-looking hiking boots and he'd *insulted* her. He had a feeling he wouldn't get very far with that apology, either.

Sometimes it was just better to cut your losses and shut up.

At Swiftwater Creek he waved toward a faint deer trail leading through a stand of skeleton-white birch. "The lake is another quarter mile that way. I've got to cross here and go about a mile to check on that missing wolf."

"Hmm." She tipped her head, considering. "Maybe I'll just go on to the lake, then."

"I'd rather we stayed together."

"That's sweet, but you said the wolves try to avoid people. Right?"

"Yes, but—"

"Then I'd rather start taking pictures so I don't hold you up. Don't worry, I did do a fair amount of hiking in Michigan on my own."

He believed it after seeing her in action. Still, he hesitated. He'd never seen another person out here, and with the midmorning sun high in the sky, few of the larger animals would be out foraging. If he moved fast, he'd be able to rejoin her in less than forty-five minutes.

"I'm a big girl, Ethan. I'll see you later."

"Wait." He swung his backpack off and searched the seldom-used side pockets. "I still have these from my last trip to Glacier," he said. He tossed her an aerosol can of bear spray, then unwrapped the clanger and also tossed her a brass cow bell. "Just make a lot of noise and sing."

"Thanks. But believe me, if I start singing, this entire forest will empty."

"Just don't terrify the wolves, okay?"

She laughed. "I'll try to be selective."

ETHAN CHECKED his current GPS position against the coordinates Frank had given him and started out on a meandering deer trail at a jog.

When the trail twisted to the south, he struck out through the brush, dodging low-hanging spruce branches and skirting tangles of wild raspberry and outcroppings of rock partly hidden by vegetation.

Every few minutes he rechecked his position on the GPS device in his hand, readjusted his direction and forged on, his progress hampered by the terrain and underbrush. In a quarter mile range of his quarry, he stopped. Listened. Sorted out the fragrances of pine and damp earth.

At the top of the next rise he dropped the GPS back in his pocket and followed the odor of wolf—typical, because of the carrion they often rolled in—the last twenty feet.

It was the yearling male he'd watched from its birth and had collared with Frank's help just last fall. A dark, blood-matted hole in its hide identified the entry of a rifle bullet.

Ethan's sense of loss bit deep. Not all the pups in a litter survived. Wolves of all ages succumbed to other wolves, to highway traffic, to mange and distemper. But this one had been a robust male with good prospects for successful dispersal into new territory until some idiot had ended his life.

Ethan released the radio collar, sealed it in a plastic bag to contain the musky wolf odor and dropped it into his backpack.

In slowly widening circles he scanned the ground for evidence. Sure enough, he found a boot heel print in a patch of mud—too blurred for further identification—which showed that the shooter had come to check out his kill.

Another ten feet away a cigarette butt lay near part of a sneaker print. Two people, then, at least one of them a smoker. From the size of the prints they were likely both males.

Which didn't rule out many suspects at all.

He pulled out his cell phone and checked for a signal. *Bingo.* Surprised at finding even a weak signal, he punched in Frank's speed dial number but only got his voice mail.

"Hey, your coordinates were right on. Rifle

shot, just as we thought. Found two sets of footprints—probably male—and a Camel cigarette butt. It was chilly enough last night that the carcass doesn't show much decomposition yet. A four-wheeler can get to the site easily, so someone needs to pick him up for necropsy."

Ethan ended the call and took a final survey of the area. "You deserved better than this," he said as he paused by the young wolf one last time. "I'm sorry."

This was government property and there was no livestock out here to defend. The killing was a senseless waste. The fact that the culprit would probably never be caught filled Ethan with anger.

Just once, I want to catch one of those guys in the act.

HE FOUND ABBY on the massive boulder overlooking the lake, kneeling with her elbows braced on the rough granite, her camera just inches from a cluster of bluebells growing out of a split in the rock.

She sat up and tugged on the bill of her cap. "Any luck?"

"Not for the wolf."

"Oh." Her smile faded. "I suppose some jerks thought they were hot stuff, killing a beautiful animal like that."

"Unless it was a livestock owner out for revenge."

"Now what?"

"The state will pick him up for necropsy. They'll check his nutritional status and overall health."

"Can they do ballistics on the bullet and find out who did it?"

He had to smile at that. "Maybe on 'Law and Order,' but it's a little beyond the scope of this situation."

The sun had turned the tip of her nose pink. Indignation brought color into her cheeks to match. "So what can we do about it?"

"The DNR can hope for a good lead. Maybe these guys will brag to the wrong person, or someone will see them the next time they're out looking for fun."

"And in the meantime, they can decimate the wolves up here and just feel really proud. That's *despicable*."

"I agree." He looked out over the lake, waiting for its beauty to fill him with a sense of calm and peace. Instead his gaze veered back to Abby.

She looked through her viewfinder at a gnarled, stunted spruce that had somehow gained a foothold in a crevice of rock. "You never really told me what you do with the wolves. I mean, I know you *watch* them, but…"

He settled on the rock next to her and watched an eagle soar high overhead. "Wolf pups are born in the spring. Usually by mid-June the pack moves among several rendez-vous sites in the area, where the pups are left while the adults hunt."

"All alone?"

"They're well hidden. This year, I've been observing this pack as much as I can, at dif-ferent times of the day. With GPS data from their collars, tracking by air and the foot-prints, I'll follow them when the snow falls. I should have a detailed history of their range and how they interact."

"And when you're working for the DNR?"

"A lot of different things. One was helping students who come north to study the wolves as part of their college program. They help do howl studies, snow tracking and radio monitoring."

"*Howl* studies?" She grinned. "That's so cute."

"It's useful, actually. The juveniles have a different pitch. It helps locate the den and gauge the success of the pack's population."

"Ah. How well they howl?"

"How many pups survive."

"Now that's just sad."

Watching the range of emotions play across her face, he felt an unfamiliar tug in his chest. *But she's leaving and you can't,* he reminded himself sharply. This is where his work was. This is where he'd inherited land that had been in his family for generations.

He launched to his feet and shouldered his pack. "We need to start back so you can get to the fairgrounds."

"I sure hope someone will have news about the theft. Maybe the guy's been caught."

"With luck, the thief wasn't very smart." He waited while she gathered her things, then started down the path. "Most of them aren't."

A gunshot reverberated through the shallow valley below and the two froze. A flock of birds rushed skyward.

The forest fell totally, eerily, silent.

"What was *that?*" Abby whispered.

He held up a hand and listened. Waited. Then he turned and saw her pale face. "I'm not sure who it was, but that was a rifle, and it's straight ahead. I think we'd better take another route home."

CHAPTER EIGHTEEN

"WHAT A WEEKEND. I kept hoping this would be over right away." Her arms folded across her chest, Erin paced Abby's office one more time before dropping into one of the chairs facing the desk. "A great way to start out a Monday morning, isn't it?"

"There's still no word?" Abby bit her lower lip. "No news after the cleanup yesterday?"

Erin shook her head. "We found the cash box in a waste can by the water fountain. Empty. There were four sets of prints on it—all from people who helped with the auction, though the best ones are yours."

"Of course they are. I brought the box to the hospital."

"Which means that either the thief was one of the four, or he wore gloves. Which, as we all know, are in plentiful supply in this setting."

Uneasy, Abby realized where this was heading.

"The sheriff questioned everyone on third shift Saturday night. He and Joe Barker searched for over an hour and then came back early Sunday morning. He also—" Erin's eyes filled with sympathy "—questioned the other three whose fingerprints were on the box. Everyone had airtight alibis for the entire night of the theft."

Abby's stomach squeezed into a tight fist. "So now I'm a suspect." She tried to quell the tremble in her voice. "Is he coming here to question me?"

"He'll be arriving in a few minutes. I'm really sorry, Abby. It's just a formality. Don't think for even a *minute* that I have any doubts."

"I'll gladly take a lie detector test, anything to clear my name." She stood and looked out the windows into the July sunshine. Canada geese strolled along the small pond at the far end of the lawn. An elderly long-term-care resident sat in a wheelchair on the patio, visiting with a relative. A normal day. Normal activities. Except a sheriff would soon walk through her door. What if he didn't believe her?

"I'm sure everything will—" Erin stared at the floor by Abby's desk. "Look."

"What?"

Mystified, Abby stood and moved to the side of her desk, then crouched to pick up a scattering of paper beneath it.

Two checks, made out to the Blackberry Hill Memorial Fundraiser.

A fifty-dollar bill.

Shocked, she stared at the money. Then she lifted her gaze to meet Erin's.

"Oh, Abby," she whispered. "Is that from the *auction?*"

"I—I didn't know it was in here." Abby sat back on her heels, her thoughts racing. "How could this be?"

At a sharp rap on the door, she looked over her shoulder and froze. Sheriff Johnson stood there, his expression grim and assessing as he stared at what she was holding.

"You found some missing money?" His voice was flat. "In your own office."

"Yes—I think so. Just now." Standing, she felt out of breath, as if she'd run for a mile without stopping. "Erin happened to look down, and there it was—under my desk."

He shifted his attention to Erin. "You knew I'd be stopping by. Did you tell Abby?"

Erin paled. "Why, yes."

"When?"

The look she shot Abby begged her forgiveness. "Just a few minutes ago. We were talking about the theft, and I thought she should know."

"Convenient discovery, then." Frowning, he reached into a leather pouch at his waist and pulled out a pair of vinyl gloves. From another he retrieved a plastic bag. "Move back, Ms. Cahill, to the opposite wall. I'd like to look through the desk, if that's okay with you?"

Abby nodded. "Absolutely."

He carefully searched the drawers and pulled a handful of checks from a hanging file.

Shock and fear turned Abby's blood to ice. Each passing second seemed to last an hour as he continued. One check after another after another.

"I had no idea. *Really.* My office door was locked that night. It always is. And…"

The sheriff held up a hand to silence her.

A lifetime later he stood. "Mrs. Reynolds, I counted fourteen checks in addition to the fifty. How much is actually missing?"

Erin bowed her head. "There should be four thousand, eight hundred and fifty in cash, based on the auction receipts. The rest of the people paid by check."

"So most of the cash is still missing." He lifted his stony gaze to Abby's face. "You have to come with me, ma'am. We need to talk, and I'd rather conduct this down at my office."

The room started to spin. "A-are you saying that I'm under *arrest?*" This had to be a joke. A crazy, far out, stupid joke. "I've never even had a *parking* ticket."

"It's no joke, ma'am." The sheriff drew up to his full height, one hand on his service belt.

Probably ready to haul out his handcuffs, Abby thought bitterly. "Don't worry. I'll come with you. But I sure hope you have a lie detector available, because this is *absurd.*"

"W-wait," Erin said faintly. "This isn't right. It can't be. If she took the money, why on earth would she hide it so badly? Someone *wanted* them to be found. And they must have hidden it here, so Abby would take the blame."

The sheriff glanced from one to the other. "Why don't both of you come with me? Oh, and feel free to look upset when you leave."

THE TWO WOMEN WALKED out together, with the sheriff behind them. But in the parking lot he told them to take Erin's car and follow him.

"I don't understand," Abby whispered. "Wouldn't you think he'd have shoved me into the back of his patrol car?"

Erin shook her head as she drove down Main. "I don't understand any of this."

Abby fell silent. None of the people here really knew her. Even with an excellent résumé and references, who would believe her? And if she was charged and convicted of a crime she hadn't committed…

She folded her arms over her pitching stomach. Was that what Erin was thinking right now? That she'd made a horrible mistake in bringing Abby here?

As they followed Sheriff Johnson into his office, Erin touched her arm. "I just want you to know, Abby, that I've never had any doubts about you and I still don't. Not a single one."

Johnson waved them toward the two heavy oak chairs facing his desk. "Abby says she arrived at a quarter after midnight, but no one saw her. When we searched the hospital on Saturday night we didn't find anything other than the empty cash box."

"So you think I went to my office and hid the money in my desk?" Her voice came out thin, hollow. Clasping her trembling hands, she felt colder than she'd ever been in her life. "Wh-why would I hide it so poorly? And why wasn't it *all* there?"

"Tell me again what you did. Step by step. With the exact times, as you remember them."

He was going to compare this version to her first, looking for discrepancies. All she could do was tell him exactly what happened and hope she didn't forget some detail. Abby took a steadying breath and recounted her trip into the hospital.

Johnson took notes, his face devoid of emotion. "You saw no one? You're absolutely sure?"

"Yes. The place was almost eerie, it was so quiet." She flinched, remembering the awful moment she'd been attacked. "I—I had no idea that someone was behind me until it was too late."

"Is it possible someone could have followed you from the pavilion?"

"The people who were there at the very end? I can't imagine any one of them being capable of this…or that stupid. The ticket sales money for the dinner dance is already in the bank. Some of the auction payments were in personal checks, which would be impossible to cash. And who could ever spend that big cashier's check for the car, made out to Blackberry Memorial?"

"There's still the matter of the missing currency—nearly five thousand dollars. That's a hefty windfall for just about anyone." He leaned back in his chair, hiked one black leather boot over the opposite thigh and tapped his pen against his mouth. "I've questioned a number of people. Two of them referred to some earlier incidents at the hospital apparently directed against you."

"Someone altered some of my documentation. Later, I believe someone tampered with an IV I'd started correctly."

"So you think someone might be trying to discredit you?"

She began to breathe a little easier. "I'm an interim director of nursing. Even if someone hated me, they all know I'm just here for the summer. Why bother?"

"Have you had to discipline anyone? Let anyone go?"

"Only the usual supervision, guidance. A verbal warning about absenteeism, but nothing beyond that." She met Erin's eyes and knew they were thinking about the same employee.

He leaned forward to brace his elbows on the arms of his chair and steepled his fingers. "Quite honestly, I initially figured you took the money. You certainly had the means and the opportunity, but I wasn't sure about the motive."

"I—"

"Wait. I did a background check on you, Abby. You've had long-term employment. A stable address, until coming here. No criminal history. And frankly, two of the staff members I interviewed were outraged when I questioned them about your actions on Saturday night." He cracked a smile. "You might have an enemy here, but you also have some strong allies."

"We've been extremely pleased with her at the hospital," Erin said. "At the last board meeting, we discussed our disappointment that she won't be here permanently."

He studied Abby thoughtfully. "Why would you take on a demanding job like this one for the summer?"

"I've been teaching for years, and wanted to update my clinical and management experience before starting a new teaching position next fall."

He nodded, as if she'd just confirmed his opinion. "I'll have a fingerprint analysis done on the currency. It's clear you'd hardly have hidden it so poorly, unless you had a burning desire to be caught."

"But if this guy had gloves on…"

"With luck, the perpetrator found it difficult to handle the paper with his gloves and took them off." The sheriff flashed a wicked smile. "People don't realize we can lift exceptionally nice prints from paper."

Erin frowned. "But if he wore gloves…"

"There'd be prints on the inside of them." Johnson's smile disappeared. "My deputy and

Joe Barker searched Abby's office while I went through yours. They obviously did a poor job of it if they missed that shelf of books, but there were no vinyl gloves found in the wastebaskets of either office."

Abby forced her clenched hands to relax. "So where does that leave me, exactly?"

"I may need to ask you more questions. For now, we're checking criminal histories on a number of people who might have had access to the hospital, including those on duty Saturday night." He quirked a brow. "By the way, an anonymous donor has offered a five-hundred-dollar reward for information leading to a conviction."

Erin stiffened. "I don't think you'll find anything on your employee criminal checks. The hospital has done background checks on every new hire for the past fifteen years. The other employees have been around for so long that we'd surely know."

"It's just part of the procedure, ma'am." He turned to Abby. "And in the meantime, you won't be leaving town. Correct?"

"Not until August thirtieth. Er, that was my plan, anyway."

"Call me if you hear or see anything suspicious." He reached inside a drawer and slid two business cards across his desk. "Given the timing of the theft and the lock system at the hospital, this was likely an inside job—someone you know and trust."

"When we left the hospital, you said we should feel free to act upset," Abby murmured.

"If someone wanted to set you up, he might hear that you were taken here for questioning. If he feels safe, he's more likely to make a mistake."

"You think there'll be more trouble?"

"I hope not. With luck, we'll find a stray fingerprint or some other piece of evidence, and it won't go any further." He stood, in a silent gesture of dismissal. "But be careful, and don't try to play detective on your own. Someone will have a lot to lose over this."

BACK AT THE HOSPITAL, Abby felt the stares as she strolled to her office. A nurse's aide peeked around a corner, her eyes round. Down a few rooms, one of the nurses tentatively waved in a weak show of support.

Some of them probably thought she was

guilty. All in all, the next five weeks were going to be a lesson in patience and humility.

But if Sheriff Johnson decided her fingerprints, means and opportunity were the best evidence he could find, things could prove to be far, far worse.

At the sound of footsteps behind her, she turned to see Gwen with a grandmotherly smile on her face. "I thought I'd try to catch you during my break," she said, puffing from the exertion. "Grace stopped by and said she hoped to see you."

Grace—just the person she wanted to see. If anyone had good advice about this, it would be the woman who'd been the guiding force in the hospital for over thirty-five years.

"When did you see her?"

"Fifteen, maybe twenty minutes ago." The affection in Gwen's voice was unmistakable. "My, she looks good. Radiant. Isn't her marriage a dream come true? I suppose she was dreading a lonely retirement. Now she has a new husband and a new home, and time to enjoy both."

"I'm happy for her, too." Abby started edging away, knowing how long Gwen could chitchat. "I'll give her a call if she doesn't stop by. Thanks."

Gwen's brows knit together. "Are you all right? You seem pale."

"Fine. Absolutely fine." Abby readjusted the shoulder strap of her purse.

"I just…well, we all want you to know that we're behind you a hundred percent. I know there's talk and all, but everything will work out."

When the older woman didn't move, Abby realized she'd probably been delegated to conduct this little fishing trip.

"I'm sure it will." Abby glanced at her wristwatch. "If you'll excuse me, I need to make some calls."

"Of course. And I'd better start setting up my med rounds." With a flustered flap of her hand, Gwen hurried down the hall.

Abby sifted through the files on her desk and pulled out a folder. One of the drug companies had promised to send out a sales rep next week to give a presentation on cardiac meds, but the woman hadn't called yet to confirm.

Abby reached for the phone, then let her hand drop. She sat back in her chair to stare at the open planner on her desk. As good a source of gossip as any, Gwen had probably already relayed that Abby appeared pale and frightened, which would feed the rumors that had to be swirling through the community by now.

At shift report, Abby would go talk to them all. And carefully watch the reactions of every person in the room.

That one of them might have set her up for arrest was a chilling thought.

"Hi, there!" Grace rapped lightly on the door before walking in.

"You get younger every time I see you," Abby teased, admiring the other woman's navy outfit and hoop earrings. "I hope you'll share your secrets. With the way things are going, I'm going to look ninety by next week."

"We walk forty-five minutes a day, eat a lot less, and I found the best thing on the internet—a face cream that does wonders." Grace smiled. "But mostly, it's just having more sleep and less stress. Which, I understand, must be a bit of an issue for you right now."

"You heard?"

"Word travels, dear, whether one tries to

avoid the gossip or not. And for the record, I stand behind you one hundred percent."

"None of this makes any sense. From the very first, it hasn't. I even went back and looked at who applied for this job, wondering if there could be resentment."

Grace snorted. "If there was, I'd think it would be directed at the woman we hired to start in September, not you. Five of our ten applicants were from this area. Once the job was filled and the new person couldn't come until fall, no one wanted to take over for the summer."

"I noticed two applicants were on staff, but aren't working here any longer."

"The Board wanted an R.N. with a bachelor's, preferably with business management course work, and none of our nurses had that. One decided to go back to college, so she'd have a better shot the next time she applied for a director of nursing position. One got miffed and quit. She moved to the Twin Cities, and I hear she was hired as a DON for a small long-term-care facility."

"Not exactly strong leads, then."

"Not really. Gwen, Carl and Marcia applied, but they just joked about it afterward.

They said it would've been tough supervising people they'd worked with as peers."

"Even Carl?"

"Ah, Carl." Grace smiled affectionately. "That boy has faced plenty of troubles in his life. He's always had a bit of a chip on his shoulder, but he's a good man."

"Financial troubles?"

"Family. He cared for his elderly parents for years before they died. Even if he'd won the job, I don't think he would've taken it. I think he's saving his money so he can go back to school in Madison or Milwaukee."

"And the other two?"

"Gwen's too rigid about 'how things have always been.' She can also be too emotional and tends to get flustered, but she's such a softy. She dotes on her dogs and cats. Marcia's a clock-watcher and can't wait to leave every day, but that's because she's so involved with her nieces' and nephews' sports. She also helps her elderly parents a great deal.

"Neither one would've enjoyed the long hours. In fact, they both seemed relieved."

Abby nodded as Grace started talking about an upcoming trip, but her words barely registered.

Grace clearly still felt loyal to her former employees. She didn't believe any one of them capable of wrong-doing.

But *someone* was. And right now, Abby's nursing license could be at stake.

CHAPTER NINETEEN

MAX HARRINGTON, one of Ethan's latest renters, propped his forearms on the top of the
gate and grinned down at the tumble of puppies wrestling in the yard.

A divorced oral surgeon from St. Paul, he
was in his late forties, with black hair silvered
at the temples and the look of someone who
spent his spare time at a fitness club...or in
front of a mirror.

"I'm not sure how much these pups will
cost," Abby said with a twinkle in her eye.
"But I'm sure they'll be *wonderful* hunters.
Maybe you need two."

Friday had been hot for northern Wisconsin, and even now, at six o'clock, the temperature was in the mid-eighties. After work
Abby had changed into crisp white shorts and
a sleeveless top, and Max was now eyeing
her, not those pups.

Ethan forced his attention back to the tackle box he'd opened on the tailgate of his truck.

Next time Max called for a reservation, the cabins were going to be full. Probably well into the next century. What kind of middle-aged guy would make a play for a much younger woman anyway? A self-absorbed, cocky, shallow—

Sharp pain lanced through Ethan's hand, jerking his attention back to the tackle box and a fishhook neatly jammed into his thumb.

A large hook, luckily…and the barb hadn't buried deep enough to catch. *Serves you right. She's not your business.*

There hadn't been a day this week when he hadn't thought about the way she'd felt in his arms after the hospital benefit. It had been hard to remember exactly why the risk seemed so great…at least, until he looked at Keifer and remembered the pain of divorce. The loss. And the way the poor kid was shuffled between parents like a piece of baggage.

He pulled out the hook and pressed his throbbing thumb against the side of his forefinger to stop the bleeding, and searched one-handed through the tackle box for a Band-Aid.

"Are you okay?" Abby called. She handed the squirming pup to Max and leaned over the fence next to him.

"I'm *fine*," Ethan muttered.

A worry line formed between her arched brows. "But you're bleeding!" She came through the gate, gently nudging the contingent of puppies away with her foot, and examined the wound. "We should wash this, then use some antibiotic salve. Who knows where that hook was last."

"Probably in the mouth of a twenty-pound walleye."

"That's awful!"

"Why? I catch and release."

"That's nice for the fish, but I *really* think we need to take care of you. When did you last have a tetanus shot?"

"Five years or so, plus a booster in June at the hospital."

Her hair smelled like wildflowers. After weeks of being outside during the late afternoons after work, her skin had tanned to bronze with a trail of freckles across her nose he hadn't noticed before. His first inclination would have been to brush off her advice, but then he caught Max's expression darkening as he looked between them.

"I thought we were going fishing. Aren't you about ready yet?"

"He'll be out in a second, Max." Abby led the way into the house and retrieved the box of first-aid supplies from a cabinet as he washed and dried his hands.

"Good boy," she teased as she applied antibiotic cream and a Band-Aid. "I wish I had some cute stickers for you to choose from."

His resolutions about keeping careful distance faded when she tipped her chin up to look at him and he saw that behind her casual humor there was also a hint of regret.

"Thanks," he said quietly. "You've been a good sport, putting up with Keifer and me."

"A good *sport?*" Her dimples deepened. "I'll take that, I guess. I know we've been avoiding each other and that it's been…awkward since last weekend."

The turn of the conversation made the back of his neck prickle. He reached into the back pocket of his jeans for his truck keys and edged toward the door. "Uh…"

"No, wait," she said earnestly. "You don't have to avoid me, really. We're just friends who briefly felt something a little deeper. Don't worry, because I'm not looking for anything more. I'm okay with things the way they are."

Maybe she was okay with it, but he wasn't.

This past week, the predatory interest of his renters toward her had rankled. And now, through the kitchen window, Ethan could see Max checking his reflection in one of the side mirrors of his pickup.

Even from here it was obvious the guy still had that avaricious gleam in his eye. "I think you should watch out for Max."

She tightened the cap on the tube of antibiotic cream and tossed it back into the first-aid box. "Why?"

"He looks like the kind of guy who plays the field."

"Really." She raised a brow.

Ethan curbed his rising impatience. "He's only here for another few days, and then he'll be gone. Maybe he's got a lot of money and sophistication, but he's the kind of guy…" He shook his head. "Forget it. You're a big girl, right?"

"Right. One easily lured by the bank account of an aging hustler who thinks *doctor* in front of his name equals a free ticket to play." She gave Ethan a look of disdain. "Go. Take the man fishing. I never make the same mistake twice."

AFTER TAKING ABBY the long way home during their walk last Sunday afternoon, Ethan had gone back to search for the person who'd fired a rifle.

The guy had disappeared without a trace.

And though Ethan had reported the gunfire to the sheriff and continued to be vigilant, he hadn't caught sight of anyone in the Lake Lunara wolf pack's territory.

He'd heard another distant rifle shot, though. And on Wednesday, he'd seen a wolf through his binoculars, one with a dark stain on its side that looked suspiciously like a trail of blood from a gunshot wound. By the time he'd hiked to the location, the wolf had disappeared, its paw prints lost in a forest floor of heavy pine needles and brush.

But now, thanks to Peter Barton's habit of keeping a pot of coffee on the stove at his feed store, Ethan knew conversations had been heating up all week over the wolves—especially after the loss of Harlan Buford's coonhound. And that sounded like something worth checking.

Keifer sat glumly on the edge of the porch. "Why can't I go, too? I thought Saturdays were supposed to be fun."

Since hearing the gunshot, Ethan had refused to let him come along. "Another time, maybe."

Keifer's lower lip jutted out. "You said that last time. You're always on the stupid computer or taking some guy out fishing or watching those dumb wolves."

It wasn't exactly true. Every day, Ethan took Keifer fishing or saddled up Buddy and let him ride…they'd been hiking.…

With every day, Ethan hoped they were forging a stronger bond…and was even more upset about the boy's imminent departure.

But it was true that Keifer didn't have friends here, other than the Reynolds kids, and the days probably dragged for him.

When Ethan was working in his home office, the boy either played with the puppies or came inside to watch DVDs and play video games.

Not living here during the school year meant he didn't have connections with the local kids, and he'd turned down Ethan's offers to enroll him in swimming or baseball or other summer sports in town.

Abby appeared on the porch and spared Ethan a glance before smiling at Keifer. "Hey, remember what we planned for this afternoon?"

The boy's shoulders sagged. "A movie."

"You still want to go, right? It's our turn to treat the Reynolds kids."

Keifer looked up at Ethan, then turned on his heel. "I guess. I got nothing else to do."

Ethan watched him trudge up the porch steps and felt a bucket-load of guilt and regret settle in his chest as he climbed into his truck and drove the five miles to the Buford place. *I promise...next week will just be for you.*

Chickens and ducks scattered as he turned off the highway onto a weed-choked lane. A half mile in, he found a clapboard house with a torn screen in the window and the door hanging ajar. A ramshackle barn listed seriously to the west behind the house.

A battered pickup with its hood up stood in the middle of a barnyard cluttered with rusting implements. The broad rear end of a man in greasy coveralls hung out over the front fender.

The frenzied barking of a coonhound chained to a tree brought the man backing out of the motor with a scowl. He hitched the strap holding up his coveralls and stood still, making no effort at hospitality. Rhythmically, he slapped the wrench he held against his opposite palm.

"Harlan Buford?"

That earned Ethan a cold stare.

"I'm Ethan Matthews."

"I know who you are." He bellowed at the dog to shut up and waited until it slunk to the far end of its chain. "What do you want?"

"I understand you had some trouble up here." When the man didn't answer, Ethan added, "I hear you lost a coonhound."

"Wolves. You thought they were a great idea, some years back." He spat a stream of chewing tobacco juice on the ground. "You lost any livestock yet? Any of your dogs?"

"A calf, though I'm guessing it was killed by another kind of predator."

"I lost three calves this spring. Woulda been good breeding stock. This week I lost a hound."

"You're sure it was the wolves?"

"DNR guy came out and confirmed it," Harlan snarled. "So I'm gonna get restitution. But that don't replace the real value of my hound. The years of training." His lips curled. "And the affection of a man for his best friend."

"The state goes by the recommendations of breeders. The kennel club. The current market."

"I said, it still ain't gonna cover what that hound was worth to *me*." The man's eyes narrowed. His voice dripped venom. "And what is it to you? You ain't working for the state now anyway, from what I hear. You got no authority—you're doing some study."

"One of the yearlings in the pack of wolves I'm studying was shot a week ago. The next day, I heard rifle fire. I'm worried about the safety of those wolves."

"Safety? That's what the *locals* got to worry about." Harlan continued to slap the wrench against his palm, his stance the stiff, alert posture of a pit bull on the verge of attack. "If you're thinking it was me, you're wrong."

"I'm just stopping by a few farms to spread

the word. The state's doing a necropsy on the carcass, and there'll be a substantial reward for any information leading to the arrest of the person responsible." Ethan forced a casual smile. "If you knew who did it, you could make a lot of money with just a phone call."

Harlan's gaze flickered. "Why would I know?"

Because it's written all over your face.

Ethan shrugged. "See you around. Sorry to hear about your dog."

One down, three to go. With the lure of a reward and the veiled warning about consequences, this trolling expedition just might scare the poacher into stopping or lead to a name.

And either would help save the Lake Lunara pack.

ON SUNDAY NIGHT Keifer belly-flopped onto his bed, picked his portable video game off the floor and started playing it for the fifth time that day.

After an entire year of being in school, he'd looked forward to being here with Dad. He'd imagined lots of adventures, just like the ones he'd read about.

He'd let his imagination run wild, and he'd conveniently forgotten that northern Wisconsin didn't exactly have mountains and canyons and wild rivers. He'd also forgotten that Dad had to work...

Keifer cut a quick glance at the darkened windows and wished there were curtains.

He'd gone to feed Dad's horse an apple last night...and had nearly run into someone standing beside the barn.

The guy had been wearing black, from his knit watch cap to his jeans, like someone out of a ninja movie. And the guy had seen *him*.

Not only seen him, but had grabbed him by the shoulders and shaken him, hard. "You never saw me, kid," he'd rasped in a harsh voice. "You tell anyone and your dog will die. And someone else here is gonna get hurt, real bad. And you know what? It could be *you*. Understand?"

Terrified, Keifer had been too stunned to speak.

The guy had given him another hard shake. "You better, because I'll know if you tell. It'll be your fault if anything happens to your dad."

And then he'd given Keifer a shove into the

wild raspberry vines growing by the side of the barn. The tiny thorns left bloody scratches that stung his hands and face, but he'd been too afraid to crawl free until he'd heard nothing but the sounds of the livestock for a long, long time.

Shivering from a cold sweat, his heartbeat still thundering in his ears, he'd slipped into the house unnoticed. He'd washed with cold water until the blood was gone and just a thin network of scratches remained, but Dad had still noticed.

So he'd lied and said he'd stumbled into the raspberries.

Ever since, his stomach had been tied in knots and he'd flinched at every sound outside. He'd nearly cried *Don't go!* when Dad went out to do chores this morning.

He knew he should tell. Maybe Dad could do something about that guy. Yet the forest was deep and dark around here, and stretched for endless miles.

If Dad called the sheriff, that guy could hide too well to be found…but he still might see the patrol car, and then he'd know that Keifer had ratted on him.

And then…

Keifer tried to concentrate on the electronic game remote in his hands. He lost control and the superhero on the screen died in a blast of gunfire from the hidden Forces of Doom.

He took a shuddering breath.

If Keifer wasn't careful, the same thing could happen for real.

CHAPTER TWENTY

AFTER HELPING WITH the supper dishes on Monday, Keifer followed Ethan to the edge of the yard. He ignored Belle, Rufus and the wiggly five-week-old puppies who were vying for his attention. "I—I don't think you should go."

"I won't be late." Ethan ruffled a hand through Keifer's hair. "And I promise you, every afternoon for the rest of this week is yours. Start thinking about what you'd like to do."

"You'll just be busy with something else." Keifer kicked at a rock and jammed his hands into his pockets. "That's okay."

"I know it's been tough this past week."

"Maybe you should stay home tonight." Keifer chewed on his lower lip. "What if it's not safe?"

"What isn't?" Ethan smiled. "I live out here, son. It's familiar ground."

"But…what if…" The boy's gaze veered away. "I mean, you don't know who could be out there."

"Have you seen someone?"

"*No.* I just figured we could do something together, like maybe…fishing. I'd really, really like to do that."

"Not tonight. But tomorrow, yes."

Abby came out into the yard and shaded her eyes against the sun. "What's up?"

Keifer glared at Ethan. "Now I know why I don't live with you," he cried. "Mom was right. You don't care if I'm here or not."

"Your mother said that?" Ethan fought to keep his voice even. "It's not true."

"I overheard her talking to her boyfriend. Why would she lie?" He took the porch steps two at a time. The kitchen door slammed behind him.

Abby watched him go, then turned back to Ethan. "Oh, dear. Not a good day?"

"Keifer doesn't want me to leave this evening." Ethan sighed. "I don't blame him. He's only got three weeks left. I just wish this summer could have been different."

"Give yourself a break," Abby said firmly. "You've done what you had to do. You had this year to complete your study, and you couldn't let that go. Right? Parents with full custody can't entertain their kids 24/7, either."

"I wanted him to have such a great time that…"

"He'd want to stay for good? It isn't his choice now, anyway. It's all set up in your custody arrangement."

"I just want him to love coming here, every chance he gets. Instead, I think he's going to dread having to ever return."

"You're a great father." She moved closer and rested a comforting hand on Ethan's arm. "He's not saying he hates being here. He just wants more time with you, because that's the best part of the day for him."

"I guess."

"And I couldn't help but hear that he's worried about your safety. Living in suburbia most of the year, he probably thinks the forest is a scary place. And that last outburst? He was just lashing out because he's upset. I wouldn't put too much stock in what he said."

Some of Ethan's tension eased. "I suppose you're right."

"Of course I am. Resident nurse and family counselor at your service, low rates." She grinned and waggled her fingers to shoo him away. "So get on your way, then. Everything will be fine here."

In the face of her calm logic, he could almost believe it would be.

"Thanks, Abby." He brushed a finger along her silky cheek. "I'm not sure who's getting the better end of our deal, but I think it's me."

"As long as you believe that, then Belle and I still have a good home. Take care, Ethan." She turned to go, then pivoted back to face him, her eyes troubled. "And do be careful. Okay? I agree with Keifer. Those woods scare me, too, sometimes. Especially when someone could be out there with a gun, who might not appreciate your stance on wolves."

A COUPLE OF THE MEN Ethan had visited on Saturday had been almost hostile about the county's wolf population. Most were philosophical, figuring that the state promptly paid the market value of any livestock lost, and with a higher population of natural predators, there'd be less deer to ravage crops.

Just one—a retired man living in a small cabin with a collection of fishing rods leaning against his front porch—had given Ethan a good lead. The past few evenings Oliver had heard rifle fire south of the lake, and thought he'd seen two or three men from a distance.

On Sunday afternoon, Ethan had searched the area and found cigarette butts, beer cans and some stray ammo on a knoll overlooking one of the Lunara pack's rendezvous sites, with bent grass showing signs of recent activity.

Someone else had apparently settled in to watch the wolves, but not with any sort of scientific study in mind.

Ethan had promptly reported in to Frank Carter—leaving a message on his answering machine—then he'd called the county sheriff, who had promised someone would look into it "early next week."

Ethan swung wide through the timber south of the lake and found a perfect spot where he could keep an eye on the knoll. Well hidden by brush, he shook out a canvas ground cloth and pulled out his binoculars and a camera with a 300mm lens.

And then he settled down to wait.

KEIFER EYED THE CLOCK on the fireplace mantel. *Nine-thirty.* Exactly three minutes past the last time he'd looked.

He shifted uneasily in his chair. The dogs had been barking a lot tonight. Just a while ago, there'd been a distant rumble of thunder.

And Dad wasn't back. Wouldn't he come back if he heard thunder? What if—

"Your turn," Abby said, handing Keifer the dice with a wicked gleam in her eye. His marker was headed straight for Park Place and a hotel, and he almost wished he'd land right on it and go bankrupt.

"Where do you think Dad is?"

"Where he always goes. Out into the timber." She tilted her head and frowned. "Are you worried?"

"It just seems like he should be back. What if it storms?"

"Your dad can take care of himself. I'm sure he's keeping a close eye on the weather."

"What if…I mean, maybe we should go check on him."

Abby laughed at that. A nice laugh, though. Warm and reassuring. "I understand how you feel, but cell phone reception is really sketchy out there, and you know what would happen? *We'd* get lost. And then he'd come home and worry about us."

Rufus and Belle started barking again, and

a shiver of fear crawled down his spine. "But what if Dad got *hurt?*"

"That's a good question. He's usually gone for about four hours. So, we'd hope he was able to make a call. But if he was *really* late, we could call the sheriff. Then the sheriff would probably gather volunteers to search for him."

But that could take hours. And in the meantime…

It'll be my fault if anything happens to Dad.

Keifer hadn't said a word. He'd been too afraid. But now the weight of that decision felt like a ten-pound sandbag on his chest. That guy wouldn't have been trespassing if he didn't already have something bad in mind.

And now Dad was out in the woods. Alone. With no idea that a stranger could be out there, wanting to cause trouble. And if anything happened to Dad, it *would* be Keifer's fault. *I should have told. I should have told. I should have told.*

Keifer halfheartedly tossed the dice and nudged his marker forward four spaces. "I'm sorta tired. Can we do this later?"

"No problem. We can leave the game set up right here." She reached over the game board and touched his forehead with the backs of her fingers. "You look a little flushed. Are you feeling okay?"

"Uh-huh. I should go out and put the pups and Rufus in the shed before it gets dark, though."

"Want me to help?"

"Nah…" He thought fast. "I think I'll play with them for a while, first."

Yawning, she stood and stretched. "I'll unload the dishwasher and then come outside, too. I'm going to miss those little dogs when they start finding new homes."

An uneasy feeling prickled at the back of his neck as Keifer hurried out, wanting to clear the yard before Abby came. It was still light enough to see. He knew the trail, so he could probably find Dad without much trouble.

He'd better not be too late.

ETHAN PROPPED HIMSELF up on his elbows and lifted his binoculars to scan the terrain below. The narrow ravine between his location and the knoll would preclude any fast pursuit should his quarry show. Still, photographing someone with a rifle raised could be enough proof for the sheriff and DNR to take action…especially if the ammunition matched the necropsy findings on that yearling.

Dusk was turning the landscape to monochromatic shades of gray and soon it would be too dark for photos. Maybe the poachers wouldn't even show.

The sharp *crack* of a branch not twenty feet away jerked his attention to full-alert.

Ethan held his breath. Brittle weeds rustled as two people came close enough for him to catch the tang of cheap beer and the smell of cigarette smoke.

"I swear, we're gonna get 'em tonight," one of the men promised. "Maybe even the whole pack."

"I want one of them pelts for my TV room. I deserve one, after what they done."

The first voice dropped to a whisper. "Shut up, or they won't come anywhere close."

Ethan cautiously moved forward a few inches and watched the men stumble down the steep bank of the ravine, then scramble up the other side to the knoll. *Bingo.*

Two of them. Big, hulking guys carrying rifles.

Hopefully, they'd see nothing to shoot at tonight.

They stretched out on the grass at the edge of the knoll and lowered their rifles in front of them. Ethan picked up his camera, zoomed in and clicked off a series of shots.

Five minutes. Ten. Fifteen.

Darkness was closing in now. He lifted the camera again and studied them through the telephoto lens. The bigger guy excitedly elbowed his companion. They slowly lifted their rifles.

Ethan snapped more pictures in quick succession, then grabbed for the .22 rifle at his side and fired twice into the air.

And hoped the wolves would scatter.

KEIFER SHIVERED and wrapped his arms around himself. Dumb idea. *Dumb, dumb, dumb.*

What had he been thinking? The beam of his flashlight was fading. The moon had slipped into the clouds and the deep, dark woods seemed to be closing in on him from all sides. The path he thought he knew so well had ended in a thicket of brambles, so he must have taken a wrong turn. And now—how could he ever get back?

He turned and tried to see where he'd been…and froze.

From somewhere ahead he heard something crashing through the underbrush. The noise stopped, then started again. And this time, it sounded as though it was heading in his direction.

He struggled to find his voice, but barely managed a croak. *"D-dad?"*

But Dad hardly made a sound when he walked in the woods. His steps were soft and sure.

His heart hammering against his ribs, he backed up. His heel caught on some sort of a branch and he sprawled over a tangle of downed limbs. His breath rasped in his throat as he scrambled to his feet and dove behind a tree.

Now he could hear footsteps. The sound of someone stumbling.

"Come on, watch where you're going!"

"If you hadn't shot that guy, we wouldn't be runnin', you fool. You and your wolf hunt."

"Hey—shut up. *Look*."

The beam of their flashlight swung past

him. Stopped. And zeroed in on Keifer's face with blinding intensity.

"It's the guy's *kid*. I've seen them together in town."

"What is he doing out here?"

"That doesn't matter. What matters is he saw us, you fool. He IDs us, and we're looking at jail time, plus Federal and state fines."

The two men fell silent.

Keifer's heartbeat thundered in his ears. They'd shot someone? *Dad?*

Cold sweat trickled down his back. With the light in his eyes, he couldn't see what they looked like, but he knew he'd never forget the harsh rasp of their voices. Low, mean, careless.

Stifling a cry, expecting the blast of a gun at any second, he twisted around and clawed at the underbrush, desperate to escape.

He stumbled, fell again, rammed into the bristly needles of a pine. Then he found his footing and ran, dodging tree limbs and vines. Behind him he heard the sounds of pursuit— heavy footsteps gaining on him with every stride.

Snapping branches.

Ragged breathing.

He swallowed back a hysterical cry when something grabbed at his arms and steadied him. "Keifer! Oh, thank God. Are you okay?"

"No! *Run!*" The words tumbled out on a wheezy breath. "Come on!" He jerked back, trying to pull free. "Men—someone's chasing me. *Guns.*"

Abby stiffened, then grabbed his hand. "This way," she directed. "Hurry!"

Somehow she found a path and they ran until Keifer's lungs were burning and each harsh breath clawed at his throat. He tripped and fell against her, and then she fell, too. They hit the damp earth in a tangle of legs and arms, both gasping for breath.

"Come *on,*" she whispered. "We've got to keep moving!"

A high-powered flashlight snapped on. And once again, the blinding light made him flinch.

"Not so fast." The voice was low, menacing, with a hint of satisfaction. "You two have gone as far as you're gonna go."

CHAPTER TWENTY-ONE

STARING AT DEATH filled Abby with an eerie sense of calm. Hyperawareness. Paralyzed in the beam of that flashlight, time seemed to stand still.

She squeezed Keifer's trembling shoulder and shifted her body in front of his. "Get ready," she whispered in his ear. "And when I touch you, you *run,* and don't you dare stop no matter what. Don't look back."

"Dad," he whispered brokenly. "They—"

"Shut up," roared one of the men. The flashlight wobbled as he stepped over a log and started toward them.

Abby balanced on the balls of her feet and rose slowly. She dredged up a bright smile. "I'm sure glad to see someone out here. We've been wandering for an hour and have no idea which way to go."

She could see the faint outline of the man's features behind the light. Younger than she'd thought, but with a chilling intensity in his eyes and a cruel twist to his mouth.

His friend moved to his side, a rifle held crossways next to his body—one hand on the barrel, one hand terribly close to the trigger. "You're farther than you oughta be, lady." He elbowed his companion and their eyes met.

The guy with the flashlight shot a quick, nervous look toward Abby. "I dunno, Dean…"

"You tell me how you want to spend the next twenty years," Dean snarled. "Me? It ain't gonna be prison for me."

He raised the rifle to his shoulder.

Something rustled in the underbrush behind Abby and Keifer. A split second later, Belle burst out, snarling and barking. Her sights fixed on Dean, she circled him, snapping at his legs as he tried to kick at her and take aim.

And then something else appeared out of the dense cover of trees behind them.

"Lonny—look out!" The gun swung wildly as a figure plowed into Dean's back. The rifle fired, fell out of Dean's grasp.

They heard an agonized scream, the keening wail rising about Belle's furious barking.

"Go!" Abby gave Keifer a hard push and

the boy had sense enough to run. She wavered, ready to follow him…

The flashlight had fallen into the weeds, its beam directed skyward. In the dim apron of light on the ground, she saw the rifle. One of the men was writhing on the ground, doubled over and whimpering.

A few feet away, nearly hidden in the shadows, the other two were locked together. She heard a sharp thud as one took a hit to the chin. A blow to his belly sent the same guy staggering. Belle darted in and tried to bite an ankle.

Abby hesitated, then lunged for the gun and quickly backed away with its barrel pointed at the two who were fighting. One of them took a blow to the jaw and fell backward.

Growling, Belle stood guard a few feet away from him, her teeth bared.

And then the only man standing slowly turned to look in her direction. *Ethan.*

"Don't shoot me," he said wearily. "It's already been a bad night."

Relief and joy rushed through her. "Keifer! It's all right!" she shouted at the top of her lungs. "*Keifer!* Your dad's here!"

She turned to Ethan. "I've got to go find

him. He could get lost out there—" And then her gaze fell to the bloodied sleeve of Ethan's shirt. "Oh, *no.*"

"It's nothing. Do you have a phone?"

"No…I lost it," she said, panicking. "I was running, trying to find Keifer…and some-where—"

"It's okay. I didn't even bother to bring mine, because half the time there's no reception out here. I can hold these two if you can go back and call 911."

"But your arm—"

"Just a graze. No big deal." He smiled wryly as he took the rifle from her and trained it on the two on the ground. "It could have been, if these two bozos had been better shots. Don't bother getting up," he added mildly, nudging the boot of the one he'd decked.

Just then Keifer appeared and rushed toward his dad, pulling to a halt when he saw the bloody shirt.

"It's okay, son. I'll be fine. Just stay back, all right?"

Abby grabbed the flashlight and pointed the beam at the guy who'd hit the ground first. He'd crawled into an upright position on the ground, his arms still doubled over his midsection. His face was ashen. "We need to get help…but I ought to take a look at this one first."

Ethan frowned. "Don't get too close. You, there, where are you hurt?"

"M-my side."

"Abby's a nurse. If you make a *single move,* if you so much as start to touch her, I swear I'll pull this trigger and I'll say it was self-defense. And just to keep things easy, your buddy will be next."

The man's gaze turned sullen.

"I'm not taking any chances on you think-ing about a hostage situation. If that isn't clear, then you can just sit there and bleed. It doesn't matter to me either way. You are," Ethan added in a dead calm voice, "no better than pond slime to me."

The man nodded and stayed still while Abby gently examined his side, then backed away. "No exit wound. This guy has quite a spare tire, and it looks like the bullet lodged in his fatty tissue. Could've nicked some bowel, but that's just a guess. We do need to get him to the E.R."

ABBY TOOK KEIFER with her and managed to find the trail leading back to the house.

In twenty minutes, the yard was filled with the flashing lights of two patrol cars and an ambulance.

The EMTs loaded Lonny Buford into the ambulance. Dean Rowley spewed threats as he recounted his injuries at Ethan's hands, but he was cuffed and shoved into the backseat of a cruiser.

Ethan refused to ride in the ambulance, so Abby called ahead and then dropped Keifer at Erin's house for the night. She took Ethan to the E.R. herself.

Marcia Larson, one of the nurses on duty, came in to clean the wound and take his vitals. "Sounds like you had an exciting night," she said. "Dr. Edwards is on duty tonight, but she's in with one of those other fellows right now. What did you all do, square off at the OK Corral?"

Ethan grinned back at her. "Not exactly."

"One of them shot at Ethan, probably afraid he'd be able to identify them. They've been trying to kill the wolves that have a den near the lake. Then one of them accidentally shot his buddy in the midst of a fight."

"Sheesh!"

Ethan shook his head in disgust. "I expect

they were afraid of facing federal and state penalties for poaching."

"So they escalated to attempted *murder?*" Marcia shuddered. "Of course, I wouldn't put anything past those boys. Just look at where they come from… Trouble as far back as anyone remembers."

From down the hall came the sound of raised voices. Someone crying out. The screech of furniture being shoved across the floor.

Sheriff Johnson's voice rose above the melee and in a moment all was silent.

"Oh, no, did that boy *die?*" Abby whispered.

Marcia snorted. "No. All the relatives showed up, for both of them. Lonny's dad is a mean one. Dean's arguing with his father and his auntie Gwen, who's none too pleased."

Abby blinked. *"Gwen?"*

"Her maiden name was Rowley. She and her brother used to run field trial dogs together when they were younger, then they started some sort of boarding and dog breeding business. I heard it turned into a regular puppy mill before it was shut down last year.

An awful place. Her brother ran the place, though. Not her."

Abby's thoughts raced back to Gwen's interest in Belle, and her mention of all the dogs she'd owned. And then to the problems Abby had experienced here at the hospital.

Ethan and Abby's eyes met. "You went out to Rowley's place last weekend," she said, lowering her voice. "Do you suppose all of this…"

"He and I go back a lot further than that, but he's not the only one I ever denied reparation."

"Did he lose cattle?"

"A couple of bear hounds he'd been training. Claimed they were worth three grand apiece." Ethan shook his head. "There were warnings in the paper that summer, week after week, telling people to avoid running their dogs within certain wolf territories. If he went ahead anyway, he was a fool. He never came up with documentation to prove those dogs even existed…and three grand is a might pricey for that kind of dog, anyway."

Heavy footsteps stopped outside the door. "You weren't happy enough, seeing me go under? Now, you've gotta go after my boy and his friends?"

Marcia shot a nervous glance at Abby. "This is Burt Rowley."

Abby stood and turned toward the door, and the blood drained from her face. The man standing there was the one who'd given her a warning during the Fourth of July street dance. The image still had the power to make her stomach pitch.

Now her revulsion turned to anger. "Those 'boys' shot this man and left him to die, which I'd call attempted murder. Your *son* held the gun that discharged and hit the Buford boy, not Ethan. And he threatened to shoot me and a ten-year-old child. You'd better have a good lawyer, because that son of yours should be sent away for a long, long time."

"You don't know what you're talking about," the man snarled. His gaze darted back to Ethan. "You've had it in for me, and I can prove it. So don't think—"

Sheriff Johnson appeared in the doorway. "We can discuss this later," he said. "I think it's time for you to go."

As the sheriff escorted him down the hall, Marcia heaved a sigh of relief. "Wow. This is almost like a big-city E.R. tonight—gunshot wounds, threats—what's this place coming to?" She patted Ethan on the shoulder. "I'll go down the hall and see what's keeping Dr. Edwards. I'm sure you look forward to being on your way."

STILL FEELING shell-shocked, Abby hovered at the coffeemaker for a moment before turning to the refrigerator and pulling out an ice cold Coke.

"I can't believe this night is over," she murmured, holding the frosty can to her cheek. "It started out just fine, and then…disaster." Outside, thunder rumbled through the sky and the wind picked up. "And now we're even getting the storm Keifer was so worried about. Or at least, that's what he claimed at the time. Now I know he was worrying the prowlers might go after you."

On the way to Erin's house, Keifer had tearfully told them about the man he'd seen lurking around the barns on Saturday night, and was sure it was the same man who'd pointed the rifle at him tonight.

Ethan tossed his keys on the counter. "Keifer kept telling me he wanted some adventure this summer. I'm just sorry he ended up with one like this."

"Believe me, once this settles down, he's going to have exciting tales to tell his buddies back home." Abby smiled, wishing she could lighten Ethan's dark mood. "After he's told the story a few times, they'll hear we fended off a battalion of villains armed with Uzis."

"Maybe so." A corner of Ethan's mouth lifted, though no humor reached his eyes. "But I'm not so sure his mother is going to be impressed."

"Crazy things can happen anywhere. *None* of this was your fault."

At the hospital Ethan's bloodied shirt had been stowed in a plastic bag, and Marcia had given him a dark green hospital top to wear home. The short sleeves revealed the stark white bandaging on his upper arm. What would have happened if Dean's aim had been just a few inches better?

Abby tried to mask her emotions with a teasing smile. "You know, you're really going to have to take better care of yourself after your private nurse leaves town. Stay away from farm equipment, guns—maybe you should get a quiet office job."

"You were amazing tonight, Abby. The way you protected Keifer and stood up to Rowley."

"Hey, I'm turning into a tough broad in my old age." After so nearly losing him, she wanted to step into his arms and feel his solid warmth, and the reassuring, steady beat of his heart.

"How's the arm?"

"It's fine. Abby, I—" He broke off. Closed his eyes. "I guess I'd better turn in. Tomorrow's already here, and I'll need to pick up Keifer first thing in the morning. He'll still be upset over all of this, I'm sure."

Ethan hesitated. He looked as if he wanted to say more, but he only turned and walked away.

AFTER A FEW sleepless hours, Abby gave up and went out onto the porch, where she settled on the big old swing and curled her legs beneath her.

The night air was soft and warm, with just the buzz of cicadas and chirping of crickets to keep her company. Peace stole over her as she reached out a toe to set the swing in motion and then curled into the pillows again.

The terrifying evening seemed like an impossible nightmare…unbelievable, in contrast to the security she now felt.

The kitchen door creaked and Ethan stepped outside. He braced his palms on the porch railing and looked up at the stars. "Beautiful night."

"Strange, isn't it? After what we've all been through?" He was dressed only in jeans and she allowed herself the luxury of taking in the long, lean lines of his back, the indentation of his spine. The white gauze and tape on his upper arm covered just a minor wound, fortunately. "You, know, I'm not sure I'd recognize you if you weren't wearing bandages."

He chuckled as he rested a hip on the railing.

She smiled up at him. "So you can't sleep, either?"

"Adrenaline overload, I guess. I keep seeing images of you and my son in front of that idiot with a gun. And quite frankly, I still have the urge to hunt him down and make sure he never sees daylight again."

Abby shuddered in agreement. "The sad thing is, those young men are now facing a long list of charges. Yet their dads were the main reason this all started, and won't face any charges at all."

"And probably won't feel any guilt about it, either."

Right after she and Ethan had left the hospital, apparently Burt Rowley and his son had ended up in a shoving match that took the sheriff and his deputy ten minutes to settle.

Burt ended up in jail in the cell next to his son's, charged with assault, disorderly conduct and public intoxication. His continuing argument with his son at the jail revealed a lot more than he might have shared if he'd been sober.

"I still can't believe it," Abby murmured. "He thought he could lie about wolves killing his dogs so he could get rich on the state reparations?"

"Not rich—but make enough to settle his debts and bring his kennel back up to code. He'd lost too much gambling at the casinos and let a lot of things slide. I remember reading in the paper about the terrible conditions in that kennel. When the state was called in for an inspection, they found dogs starving, and a lot of them were dead. Later, there were rumors that Burt abandoned the others to just run loose and die." He shook his head. "But even if he was in financial trouble, I still couldn't have verified a false claim."

"And all this time he blamed you because he went bankrupt, and he told everyone about the lousy DNR guy who cheated him."

Belle, who'd been curled up on a blanket at the end of the porch, came over to the swing, her nails clicking on the wood-plank flooring. She rested her head on Abby's lap.

Dean Rowley had admitted his dad had put him up to vandalizing Ethan's place a number of times—including tampering with the auger that broke and sent Ethan to the hospital. He'd been responsible for Belle's disappearance, as well, because the fact that one of his dogs lived with an "enemy" had stuck in Burt's craw.

"Poor Belle, at least we know where you came from. No wonder you didn't like that nasty guy earlier tonight. Bad memories, right?"

Her tail wagged slowly.

Ethan watched them, his back to the moon-lit landscape, his face cast in shadow so she couldn't quite make out his expression. "Penny for your thoughts?"

"I'm just sorry you got mixed up in all of this," he said.

"But Keifer's safe, and we're okay. I'd say we're pretty lucky." She patted the cushions. "Sit. Since neither of us can sleep, we can at least try to relax."

He hesitated before dropping next to her onto the seat. After a moment he put his arm around her and pulled her closer, and she nestled into his warmth.

He smelled of soap, toothpaste and a faint woodsy aftershave. And the solid breadth of his chest made her feel more safe and secure than she'd felt in a long time.

"This is just about perfect," she murmured, staring out at the silvery moonlit forest.

He brushed a kiss against her hair. "Absolutely perfect...and I don't think I ever really appreciated it, until now."

CHAPTER TWENTY-TWO

IT FELT STRANGE, walking into work the next day.

The floors gleamed, like always. Beth offered a cheery wave and hello, just as she did every morning.

A couple of patients were strolling along, guiding their wheeled IV stands. Down in the TV room, Abby could see a few of the old folks sitting in their padded recliners.

The sheer normalcy of it all was so jarring, so surreal, that she headed straight for her office, closed the door and had to lean against it with her eyes closed just to catch her breath.

The moment of peace didn't last long.

Her phone rang, the pharmacy paged her over the loudspeaker and then Erin appeared at her door. Abby waved her in as she finished the call.

"I heard," Erin said simply. "And I'm so sorry. Are you okay?"

"We were all lucky. Believe me."

"I thought you'd want to know that Lonny Buford was discharged into the sheriff's custody this morning, so you don't need to worry about him being here."

"How's his wound?"

"Superficial, so he'll be fine. Though after what he and his buddy did, I'm not sure he deserves such good luck. Keifer had quite a story to tell us about what happened last night."

"It's been hard to concentrate on anything else, believe me."

"There's something else you should know." Erin lowered her voice. "The sheriff was in this morning and asked us all a lot of questions. Right afterward, he took Gwen back to his office."

"Gwen?"

"After the Rowleys' accusations, he apparently wanted to take another look into the silent auction theft. I suppose he thought it was just too much of a coincidence." Erin rested her hands protectively on the swell of her belly. "He called me a few minutes ago."

Abby gripped the edge of her desk. "And?"

"I can hardly believe it, but Gwen has just

confessed to the theft of the money from the fundraiser. She's also admitted to tampering with records here. To discredit you."

"Gwen?" Abby stared at her. "But why?"

"She and her brother lost a lot of money and a good part of their livelihood when their kennel closed last year. She'd probably watched for an opportunity to take the auction money and then used it to her full advantage."

"But those altered medical records were found a good three weeks earlier!"

Erin shrugged. "The sheriff figures she was laying the groundwork, so you'd be a prime suspect."

"And then she planted part of the fundraiser proceeds in my office so I'd take the blame."

"Exactly. The sheriff got a search warrant this morning and recovered the rest of it at her place."

Relieved, Abby leaned back in her chair. "Why didn't I guess?"

"She fooled us all, Abby. Even Grace. You just never know." Erin smiled sadly. "At least there'll be no suspicion following you when you leave us. You certainly never deserved it, and we've been very lucky to have you."

ABBY HAD SEEN a lot more than friendship in Ethan's eyes the night he'd been shot.

This, of course, in the wake of facing two men who would have shot them all with no more compunction than if they'd been swatting a fly. Ethan's feelings were all about subsiding adrenaline and not what he truly felt for her. She was sure of it.

Emergencies did that—they heightened emotions, drove people to do impulsive things.

But now, as she helped Keifer pack his things, she felt a wave of sadness beyond the fact that she'd miss him after his mom arrived in a few hours to take him back to Minneapolis.

"You're a very cool kid," she said, handing him another stack of video games. She watched him put them in his duffel, then handed him another set. "I hope you know how much your dad loves you. He'll miss you."

He nodded, keeping his eyes averted. "I'll miss him, too."

"But you'll get to come back over one of the holidays, right? And next summer?"

He nodded again.

"These last couple of weeks sure flew by." She lifted his chin and smiled. "I'll miss you, too. I've never been a mom, but if I ever have kids, I hope they turn out just like you."

He dropped his videos and launched into her arms for a long, silent embrace.

After a moment she held him at arm's length. "Have you decided between those two puppies, yet?" Ethan had sold the others and kept his two favorites. "I'm glad I don't have to choose."

Ethan appeared at the door. "Your mom just pulled in the drive, son. Are you ready?"

"She wasn't supposed to come until noon!" Keifer blinked and looked at the pile around him. The projects he and Ethan had made out of wood in the shop. Piles of clothes and books. The new pet carrier Ethan had brought home yesterday.

"I'll tell you what—you go out to meet your mom, and I'll take care of your suitcase, okay? It won't take me long, and I'm sure she can't wait to see you." Abby sat back on her heels and watched the boy leave, and felt an unfamiliar tug at her heart. "It's not going to be the same without him."

"Never is," Ethan said on a long sigh. "I just count the days until the next holiday. It's one reason I've never felt compelled to remarry. What then? More kids shuffled between parents who can't get along?"

"Not all marriages fail."

"Then why haven't you tied the knot?"

"Poor choices. Bad timing. My parents were married fifty-six years, though, and my grandparents almost sixty. I know the brass ring is out there somewhere." But the words sounded hollow, even to her. "I'll finish up here, if you want to go talk to Barbara."

JUST WHAT HE WANTED to do. Ethan clenched his jaw and strode through the house, arming himself for battle.

Barbara didn't disappoint, from her first aloof glance. "Where on earth are his good tennis shoes? This isn't the brand I usually buy."

Keifer glanced between them, his tension visibly rising. "I lost a shoe, Mom. The first day. These are the new ones I wanted, so Dad bought them. I *begged* him."

Ethan's stomach twisted at his son's earnest effort at smoothing waters that would never be calm, because no one on earth had ever quite met Barbara's standards.

"I'm here a tad early, and that means we can make it back to Minneapolis in good time." She opened her arms and gave Keifer a kiss and a hug. "It's great to see you again, sweetie. I hope you were able to find enough things up here to keep you busy?"

Implying, as she always did, that northern Wisconsin was at the end of the earth.

"It was great, Mom. I can't wait to come back again."

"Really." Barbara's attention veered toward the porch, and Ethan looked over his shoulder to see Abby sidestepping out the door with a duffel bag slung over her shoulder and the dog kennel and a suitcase in each hand. She raised a brow. "How nice. Valet service."

Ethan gritted his teeth. "Keifer, go help Abby with your things. You can put it all in your mom's trunk and backseat."

Barbara's gaze hardened. "I trust you didn't spend the summer introducing our son to an inappropriate situation. This is just *soooo* like you."

He counted to ten. "If memory serves, it wasn't me who found someone else while we were married. And no, not that it's your business, there's been nothing going on here at all. Abby works at the hospital, and she needed a place to live for the summer."

Barbara huffed out a short breath.

"Look, I don't want to argue. It's tough on Keifer, and we should be beyond all of this now. He tells me you're engaged, by the way. Congratulations."

The hard line of her mouth softened. "*Almost* engaged."

Keifer bounded out of the house with two brimming brown paper grocery sacks. He stowed them in her car, then ran over to his parents and skidded to a stop.

"Abby is bringing out the last of it. Wait till you see this, Mom!" He raced to the edge of the yard and opened up the toolshed door. Rufus and Belle bounded out and chased each other around the yard. The puppies gamely tried to catch them, then gave up and started wrestling on the grass. "Aren't they *cute?*"

Barbara's hand flew to her mouth as the adult dogs peeled around the corner of the house and ran past her, nearly brushing against her white dress.

The puppies, sensing a newcomer, left their wrestling to bounce over to her. They jumped up and planted their paws against her skirt hem, wriggling for attention.

"No, *please.*" She blanched and took a step

back, wobbling when her high heel sank into the grass.

"Keifer," Ethan warned.

The boy lifted them up in his arms, where they squirmed until they could lick his face. "So what do you think, Mom? Which one?"

Her eyes looked a little wild. "I—I—"

"They'll be much quieter when they get a little older," Ethan said. "And it will be different when they're alone. He's really got his heart set on this, Barbara."

She took a deep breath. "I, um, don't think this is going to work out, Keifer. These pups are going to grow into big dogs that need a lot of space. We have a condo and just a very small yard of our own. And I have to do a lot more traveling next year. What would we do with a dog?"

"I can walk him, every day. And I'll do all the chores and…" Keifer swung toward Ethan. "And if we had to board him a long time, maybe we could send him up here? *Please?* I *love* being here. I could come more often to visit and everything!"

Ethan met Barbara's troubled eyes. "It probably is too much for you, really. I shouldn't have given in. I can just keep his favorite pup here, so he can see it when he visits." He looked down at Keifer. "The dog would be yours, son. I could email pictures, and you'd still get to see him."

Barbara gave a weary wave of her hand. "No. We'll give it a shot."

"Yesss!" Keifer pumped his fist, his face filled with joy.

"But I can't promise anything, understand? Puppies chew and make a lot of messes and they're rambunctious. And when they grow up, well—we'll just have to take this day by day."

For the first time in years, Ethan wanted to give her a hug. He ruffled Keifer's hair and mouthed a silent *thank you* to her over the boy's head. "Now, you have to choose which one—Darby or Cinder."

"I want them both so bad." He bit his lower lip. "Darby, I guess."

"How about if I keep Cinder, then? He'll be your dog, but just for up here. Deal?"

"That's *way* cool!"

Barbara looked at her watch, then she edged closer to Ethan and lowered her voice. "I don't have time to talk right now, but we need to discuss custody issues. I'm going to be traveling out of the country a lot in the next few years. I'm not sure I can keep him so much of the time anymore."

"Nothing would make me happier than to have him with me, Barb."

"Good. I'll have my lawyer contact yours in a week or two."

"The sooner, the better. Give me a date, and I'll come after him."

Her expression turned wry. "I'll miss him, too, you know. But I've realized that I haven't been entirely fair over the custody thing. Instead of being selfish, I need to think about what's best for him. And it isn't letting a housekeeper raise him while I travel and he's longing for his dad."

Stunned, Ethan stared down at her. "Thank you."

After Barbara got in her car, Keifer came to Ethan for a fervent, final hug, his eyes welling with tears. "Mom says I can come here more…if you want me."

"*Want* you? I would give anything to have you here all the time, and I'll be counting down the hours until you can come back. I love you, buddy."

"Love you, too." After another hug and a brief whirlwind of activity, Keifer got in the car.

An old familiar emptiness started to settle in Ethan's chest as the vehicle disappeared down the driveway—part of the cycle of anticipation, happiness and loss that always surrounded his son's visits. Only now, there was also joy.

Because, finally, things were going to change.

ABBY LOADED THE last of her bags into the trunk of her car, dusted her hands off against her jeans and shaded her eyes with one hand. Keifer had left a week ago, and Ethan was nowhere in sight.

"I should have guessed," she muttered to herself. "Now even Belle is gone."

If she was going to make it to the first motel reservation of her trip by evening, she needed to make tracks.

The regrets and the empty place in her heart were feelings she was determined to leave behind.

She turned slowly, scanning the edge of the forest. The lane. The fenced yard.

And then suddenly, Ethan came around the side of the house with a bright explosion of pink trotting beside him. Clearly fresh from a beauty appointment at Della's Doggy Boutique, Belle wore a big pink bow on her collar. Ethan carried a tall gift-wrapped box in his hand.

"How sweet of you," she murmured when they came to a stop in front of her. Only then did she realize that Belle wore no leash, yet she'd stopped and sat by Ethan's side when he halted.

Ethan winked at Abby and flashed a quick grin. "We have to show off, for a minute."

He stepped in front of Belle and signaled with his hand, then pivoted and walked a good thirty feet away.

Belle sat perfectly still, her gaze pinned on Ethan's face. When he signaled, she flew to him, whipped behind his legs and sat at his side, just as before.

And when he walked back to Abby, the dog trotted jauntily at his side, her tail wagging. They stopped in front of her and once again Belle sat.

"*Wow.* I didn't know she had any sort of obedience training!"

Ethan grinned down at the dog at his side. "She didn't. But she and I discussed it, and decided that we needed to do this so we could prove a point. We've worked hard all week."

Mystified, Abby looked down at the dog again. "Prove a point?"

"About old dogs and new tricks." He moved his hand and Belle dropped to the ground, her front legs stretched out in front of her and her head tilted up so she could watch his face. "Some of us let the past change everything that comes along in the future. For Belle, she's been afraid to trust, because she was hurt once before. But the right home makes all the difference for a dog like her. When you adopted her, you saved her life."

Abby stared at him, not quite daring to guess where this was leading.

"Sometimes people are just as afraid to take chances. They decide it's easier to hold back." He handed her the package and took a deep breath. "I know you've been looking forward to traveling throughout the West, and that you have a wonderful job waiting for you in California. Everyone should follow their dreams. But I thought that someday you might look back on this summer and miss a little of what you had here."

She hesitated, then carefully removed the big, glittery silver bow and wrapping paper. Lifting off the lid of the box, she caught her breath at the sight of the sparkling, crystalline tip of something peeking through the dark blue tissue paper.

And in that instant, she knew what it was. "Oh, my," she breathed as she withdrew the sculpted wolf, its nose raised and mouth open to howl, pup at its side. "It's absolutely stunning!"

It was the wolf she'd admired at the silent auction a month ago. A sculpture she'd barely dared touch because of its exquisite beauty. "I can't believe it. You shouldn't have, really. But I *love* it. How did you know?"

A corner of his mouth lifted. "I saw your face when you looked at it on the day of the auction."

"But the bidding…I would have seen your name on the invoice."

His dimples deepened. "Connor had his lab tech take care of it, so you wouldn't recognize the buyer's name."

Beyond the expense, he'd taken care to keep it a secret, and then he'd saved it for this moment. It was all so sweet and thoughtful of him that her eyes started to burn.

"I just don't know what to say." She placed it back in the box with great care, then put the box in the trunk of her car, cushioned between a sleeping bag and a soft duffel bag filled with linens. Once it was safe, she turned and wrapped her arms around Ethan. "Thank you. For everything."

He held her close, her head tucked beneath his chin. "I'll be here, if you ever head back this way."

His words curled around her heart. His strong arms around her filled her with a sense of warmth and completion.

But it was the depth of his emotion that made her forget the luggage she'd packed, the car that was running and the road map she'd left on the front seat.

And when he finally lowered his mouth to hers for a long, exquisite and breathtaking kiss, she knew she didn't need to travel to find adventure or to start a new job to fill the emptiness in her life.

Everything she'd ever dreamed of was right here, in Ethan Matthews's arms.

* * * * *

LARGER-PRINT BOOKS!

GET 2 FREE
LARGER-PRINT NOVELS
PLUS 2 FREE
MYSTERY GIFTS

Love Inspired

Larger-print novels are now available...